Praise for
Malay Sketches

Longlisted for the 2013 Frank O'Connor International Short Story Award

"The first time I read *Malay Sketches*, I was intrigued by the dialogue Alfian Sa'at had created between a pre-modern colonialism and a postmodern empathy. The second time I read it, I admired its pitch-perfect language and the warm but acute understanding of characters who do not represent ideas, but live individual lives. Alfian is less the promise of a new generation of post-colonial writers than he is the leading edge of transition to an exciting and contemporary national literature of Singapore."

> —Harold Augenbraum, Franke Visiting Fellow
> at the Whitney Humanities Center of Yale University and
> former executive director of the National Book Foundation

"Terse and profound, deliciously local and specific and thus absolutely relevant to us all now, *Malay Sketches* opens us up to a world we need to know. A huge pleasure and a must read."

> —Gina Apostol, author of *Gun Dealers' Daughter*

"Afian Sa'at's *Malay Sketches* offers a nuanced and moving portrait of Singapore's Malay community. With a beguilingly light touch, Alfian tackles weighty matters of race, class, gender, and language. These quicksilver sketches, often quietly humorous and always compassionate, are a deep pleasure to read and ponder. By turns rueful, dejected, fierce, disgraced, uplifted, baffled, and more—there's so much life here!—Alfian's characters are memorably real. This is a charming, incisive, and graceful book."

> —Martha Cooley, author of *Guesswork* and *The Archivist*

"Deft and sure-footed, these short, sharp pieces function both as necessary jibes in the face of mainstream complacency, and as a tender, clear-eyed evocation of the Singaporean Malay experience."

> —Jeremy Tiang, author of *State of Emergency*
> and *It Never Rains on National Day*

"The title is the key. Alfian Sa'at uses the name of a late-nineteenth-century colonialist project to frame a body of vignettes exposing the systematic politicization of race, the socialization of the Malays, and the individual Malay's struggle to preserve a knowledge of community in modern Singapore. Cognitively exacting books—with such fragile themes—come once in a lifetime . . . . *Malay Sketches* is an unambiguous trailblazer."

> —Gwee Li Sui, literary critic, poet, and graphic artist

"Alfian's vignettes of Singapore Malay life are touching and funny, at once full of pathos and nostalgia. They illuminate a life that once was, and now, inevitably, with 'progress,' what is. But ultimately they speak of dignity, quiet and undiminished."

—Datin Paduka Marina Mahathir,
columnist, activist, author of *In Liberal Doses*

"Through his vivid sketches of a spectrum of characters, readers will gain rare insights into the Malay psyche as an ethnic minority in Chinese-dominated Singapore . . . . Like an artist who could capture an evocative scene or a haunting portrait with just a few bold strokes of the pen or pencil, Alfian only needs a handful of words and phrases to make his characters and their dilemmas leap out of the pages to . . . illumine delicate issues."

—Ismail Kassim, former senior correspondent at *The Straits Times*

"*Malay Sketches* is a refreshingly honest and insightful depiction of the less savory realities of life in Singapore, an ostensibly multiracial and meritocratic city-state uncomfortable with its historical Malay core. The stories serve as a stark reminder of a complex and contradictory society that is at once dynamic and dastardly, progressive and oppressive, glittery and ghoulish."

—Lily Zubaidah Rahim, associate professor at
University of Sydney, author of *The Singapore Dilemma*

"These lingering vignettes, told in Alfian Sa'at's characteristically poetic cadence, disclose a hidden history unlikely to find space in the panegyrics of a state-sanctioned, ascriptive multiculturalism. Alfian records a truer account of an anxious settler community's efforts to relocate an indigenous people to the margins (and then rebuke their marginalization). It is the narrative of displaced native peoples the world over."

—Vincent Wijeysingha, lecturer at SIM University

"Subtle, delicate, elliptical, these elegiac sketches are shot through with yearning and brightness ... There are stories of separation and reunion, of love and conversion, of nation, class, childhood, gods, angels, death, and prayer. There is humor and pathos but above all a longing for something forgotten, something lost."

—Jo Kukathas, artistic director of The Instant Café Theatre

"A provocatively powerful and brutally honest work that speaks about the subject of race."

—Laremy Lee, *Quarterly Literary Review Singapore*

"Although *Malay Sketches* can be seen as a peephole into the Malay psyche, the stories will be relatable to readers, no matter their country or ethnicity. Stories of love, sadness, betrayal, and success and failure make this collection accessible and, most importantly, human."

—Goh Cheng Fai Zach, *Cha: An Asian Literary Journal*

MALAY
SKETCHES
STORIES

ALFIAN SA'AT

Foreword by Isrizal Mohamed Isa

Malay Sketches
    Text © Alfian Bin Sa'at, 2012

First published by Ethos Books, Singapore, 2012
First Gaudy Boy edition, USA, 2018

Published by Gaudy Boy, LLC, New York,
an imprint of Singapore Unbound
singaporeunbound.org/gaudyboy

For more information on ordering books, contact
jkoh@singaporeunbound.org.

ISBN 978-0-9828142-3-9

Cover design by Flora Chan

For Adriyanti Sʊ'at

"The tale of these little lives is told. If I have failed to bring you close to the Malay, so that you could see into his heart, understand something of his life...then the fault is mine."

—Frank Swettenham,
Governor and Commander-in-Chief
of the Straits Settlements

Also, author of *Malay Sketches*, published in 1895.

Contents

Foreword

On my last reading of these Malay sketches by Alfian before attempting this foreword, an absurd thought slowly formed in my mind. What if I am called upon to bear witness to the existence of these characters in the pages that follow? That is, to testify if these characters had any basis in reality or if they were mere constructions borne out of an isolated creative writing process. Amusing myself, I began to replace some of the characters' names with real-life names and could see, in these stories, real people—persons I know who had gone through situations and experiences similar to the characters. Some characters could even fit multiple real-life persons.

Here, I want to add that I do not take the term 'witness' lightly. Bearing witness is an act of conscience. I wasn't sure who the judge sitting in my head was supposed to be, to whom I was trying to attest the veracity of these characters and their stories. In the end, I was left with a sense of guilt that I had yet to attempt writing the kind of stories as Alfian has written—sketches, portraits that could expand another person's field of vision or deepen his or her regard for a community.

The circumstances of the 'making' of this volume of *Malay Sketches* deserve mention. Malay writing and publishing output in Singapore were especially prolific between the nineteenth and first half of the twentieth centuries. One of the more interesting details found in the covers of publications from this period was the exact conditions of when and where these writings were produced. Such information was sometimes added posthumously to later editions of these publications. These brief biographical sketches of the writers or publishers provide a reader—even one reading a few decades or a century later—a deeper understanding of the society, the writer's milieu of that moment and a more holistic appreciation of the work.

Back to the 'making': I recall, one night after a meeting, Alfian decided to come back to my place at Perumal Road to hang out and continue our conversations. This evolved into an extended stay, which we jokingly called 'a residency'. This was a reference to the fact that my house, in its previous incarnation, had served as an arts space which had a regular residency programme and which used to host various tenants. Alfian's 'residency' took place over a few months in two halves, broken by a period of him going across the Tebrau Straits. In my mind, this mirrored the changing landscape of the stories in this book.

For this 'residency', he had decided to use a spare bedroom in my house to write. This he did furiously and intensively. My partner (the third person in the house) and I bore witness to a friend at work. In between bouts of furious and intensive writing, there were the kitchen conversations where we would talk about this and that in the course of which we would bounce ideas around. Sometimes I would come out of my room, ranting about a news story I had come across or raving about a nugget of information I had unearthed from my web-crawling (and I do spend a lot of time excavating the borderless, bottomless Internet). Some of them, I suggested as story ideas to Alfian. Other times, he would blahblahblahblahblah and we would discuss the underlying issues, get into squabbles or similarly sink into quiet reflective moments. Occasionally, we would imagine wildly, coming up with concepts for musicals. After these shared times and exchanges, we would enter separate rooms—back to writing for him and back to reading for me.

From the outset, Alfian had always intended to write the sketches as ultra-short pieces. This meant that after a writing spurt, whatever he produced was almost immediately put up online for his (Facebook) friends to read. This process was repeated: inside room, write, outside room, talk, back to room, write, then online publishing. It wasn't all that regimented, as the regular organisation of hours into day and night was often ignored. Moreover, we sometimes continued conversations when we had returned to our rooms—that is, as online chats that were occasionally punctuated by either or both of us coming out of the room to laugh or exclaim face to face. I was rather amused by all this while observing his other habits, as he probably did mine.

There were times when I felt that maybe this was how it was in the heyday of Malay writing and publishing, albeit not in one's private domicile, rather at an office of sorts. This was an office with friends or like-minded individuals at work, creating different forms of writings to give voice to the community for wider consumption. These days, the spaces and platforms for such writings have diminished somewhat in Singapore. Taking into account the sheer pace of changes that have been taking place in Singapore (and Malaysia too) since the time we first got to know each other, the urgency for more of such writings to be produced is more acute than that felt by the generation who faced similar yet differently configured pressures arising from rapid urbanisation and modernisation of Singapore in the period of colonial rule leading up to independence.

Stories such as these are important entry points into a conversation that has yet to be held away from the realm of officialdom. Honest, open conversations about issues that are pinning down certain segments of the community whose voices appear already muffled. Alfian does not shy away from setting some of his sketches within complex, intricate circumstances of detention without trial, terminal diseases (an allusion to HIV), class disparity and race relations for instance. Yet he manages somehow to let those voices be heard or raise questions through the characters' interactions, no matter how resigned they are to the absurdity of the circumstances they are caught in, at times desiring justice and at the very least, simply querying but always with an air of dignity.

The reference to the original 1895 volume of *Malay Sketches*, by British Resident-General Frank Swettenham, is purposefully harnessed by Alfian. There is, however, another author who wrote on the same Malay community in that century, a little earlier than Swettenham. In contrast to Swettenham's observations from the outside, the author who is only known as Tuan Simi was writing what his own eyes, as someone from within, had witnessed. In 1831, he protested the fate of the Malays in Singapore under the British via a popular Malay poetry form which is sung (not spoken) termed syair. It is not known how widely disseminated the syair was.

Sampai hatinya sungguh perintah sekarang

> memberi kecewa pada sekaliannya orang
> berlainan sekali dahulu sekarang
> susahnya bukan lagi sebarang-barang.

From Syair Potong Gaji*

> How heartless are today's rulers
> who bring despair to everyone
> how different it is now from before
> the hardships are no longer ordinary ones.

From Syair On A Salary Cut

As much as Tuan Simi tried to capture the anxiety of his times through his verses, so does Alfian through his *Malay Sketches*. And just as Tuan Simi probably understood that some form of collective action was needed to alleviate the situation of his fellow men in his time, so too must we find our best step forward. Reading these sketches is as good a start as any.

Isrizal Mohamed Isa

March 2012

*Muhammad Haji Salleh (ed.), *Syair tantangan Singapura abad kesembilan belas*, Kuala Lumpur: Dewan Bahasa dan Pustaka, 1994.

The Convert

Jason wanted the whole works for his wedding. Hawa, his wife-to-be, was actually nervous about having the bersanding ceremony, where bride and groom would sit side by side on a dais. She thought that too much attention would be focused on the fact that he was a Chinese man, dressed in traditional Malay garb.

However, when they were choosing her bridal baju kurung°, Jason had marvelled at the exquisite designs on the songket°. Hawa told him, "The silk is from the Chinese, the gold threads from the Indians, and the craftsmanship is Malay."

"Do I get to wear it too?" Jason asked, clearly excited.

"Muslim men can't wear silk. But you can have the cotton songket to wrap around your waist."

"And do I get to slip in a keris° too? With the handle sticking out at the waist? I've seen it in photos."

"Don't be ridiculous. What for? You want to circumcise yourself under your songket is it?"

For the akad nikah° ceremony, Jason had memorised the words he was to say in one breath, while shaking the hand of his father-in-law. It could have been uttered in English, but Jason wanted to impress his prospective parents-in-law by doing it in Malay.

"I, Jamal Bin Abdullah (his Muslim name), receive the hand of Hawa Bte Iskandar, with a dowry of $200, in cash." The kadi*, a stern-looking man, made him repeat the line, but this time replacing the word 'ringgit' with 'dolar'. Jason glanced at Hawa, who had taught him the words the night before. She blushed, realising her mistake. Jason sped through his second attempt with ease, and there were smiles all around.

A few months later, Jason was informed by his superior that he was to be transferred to another unit. No explanations were forthcoming. He was told that he could still keep his First Sergeant rank, but that he would now be trained as an Infantry Specialist.

"But I'm a Combat Engineer," was all Jason could say, blinking at the letter in his hands. His superior sighed, avoiding Jason's eyes, and said, "It's a directive from Manpower. But you shouldn't worry, you'll still be getting the same pay."

It was only later that night, lying beside his sleeping wife, that Jason thought of an answer to his superior: "I never went around telling all of you to call me 'Jamal'. I'm still Jason." But was he? He turned towards his wife and kissed the back of her neck. She stirred and curled her back to rest in the concavity of his body.

Two years later, in an editing room, a producer was reviewing rushes to be used for a montage for the National Day Celebrations. Ordinary Singaporeans were asked to respond to the question, 'What will you defend?' A yuppie-type with black-framed glasses said, 'My job.' A scout hesitatingly said, 'My future?' A woman at a food court said, 'Myself'. And then Jason appeared on the monitor. He was wearing his army uniform, with his green infantry beret. He stared straight into the camera, and in a slow, measured tone, said, 'I will defend my family. My beautiful wife, and my one-year-old son.'

The producer thought this was the most heartfelt and sincere testimony, and slotted it right at the end of the montage. It helped that one could almost detect tears filling up the soldier's eyes.

Losing Touch

Last Saturday, at a Prize-Giving Ceremony for Top Malay-Muslim Students, I had walked up the stage to collect my scroll. Everything went as we had rehearsed, up till the moment I was face to face with the President. Suddenly I froze, snatched the scroll from the tray held by the girl beside him, and left his hand frozen in mid-air.

Of course, the protocol was that I should shake his hand. But I was wearing my baju kurung, and a tudung°. The President is a man, and I'm not supposed to have any physical contact with the opposite sex. That's a kind of protocol too.

It was difficult to bring people around to my point of view. My mother said I had "shamed the whole community" with my "rudeness". My father said, "When you do something like that, it's so easy for them to call us extremists". My sister said, "You dishonoured the guest-of-honour".

I didn't know how many people in the audience thought the way my family did. I made my sister describe what the scene looked like to her.

"You made him look so stupid", she said. "He was reaching out his hand, smiling so proudly."

"Proudly?"

"Yah what, you were the only girl wearing a tudung among all the students. He probably thought, oh, this is a girl who can balance between studies and religion. And then you had to spoil everything."

"So what did the audience think?"

"People were shocked. He really looked stupid. His one hand sticking out. Like the Kentucky Fried Chicken Colonel, you know, but just one hand lah. Some people didn't know whether to continue clapping or what."

So overnight, I became this poster girl for Malay non-integration. Apparently the President, in his memoirs to be written years down the road, would one day describe how Malays had become more and more fundamentalist, just because a panicky girl one day decided not to shake his hand. As damage control, my sister suggested that I write a letter to the President. I showed her the first draft.

"You're not apologising," she said. "You're justifying what you did."

"No I'm not. I'm educating him."

She rolled her eyes. "You nak* educate the President? Who are you?"

I wrote a second draft, this time removing the parts that argued that the handshake wasn't even part of our culture. I toned down all the rhetorical bits that began with 'you, as a fellow minority member, should'. I focused on the fact that I had never meant to offend.

When I reached the post box later that day, I found myself confronted by two different slots: 'Singapore' and 'Other Countries'. It made me pause for a while. My sister had asked who I was. What kind of country did I see myself living in? What kind of country did I want for myself? I wasn't different for the sake of being different. And being different is not the same as being difficult.

I rested the envelope on the lip of the slot that said 'Singapore'. I'll describe the scene for you. There is a girl standing in front of a post box. She is wearing a baju kurung and a tudung. An envelope has just dropped, like a leaf, from her fingers.

But she is still standing, her hand frozen in mid-air.

Three Sisters

Anisah was woken up by the sound of roosters crowing hoarsely outside her window. She opened her eyes and was startled: a green web had been spun over her while she was sleeping. She blinked hard, and realised that it was a mosquito net, suspended from a hook on the ceiling.

Her mother walked into the room and frowned.

"Wake up Anisah," she said. "Mak° Long has made jemput-jemput° for breakfast. It's not going to taste nice when it's cold."

The night before, when they first arrived, Anisah's mother had given her instructions on what to do in the bathroom. There was no shower, but there was a tub of water, made by walling in a portion of the bathroom with bricks that were later tiled. Anisah scraped the water's surface with the scoop. She gazed, fascinated, at the undulating patterns of light that were thrown on the wall.

"Who's inside?"

It was Mak Long's son, Aidil, at the door. Anisah wanted to say her name, but felt awkward; it suggested a familiarity with the boy.

"It's Mak Ngah's daughter."

The words felt very strange coming from her mouth. She had never heard her mother referred to as 'Mak Ngah' back in Singapore. Her mother was the middle one — 'tengah' — in a family of three sisters, and hence the name. The eldest, or sulung, was Mak Long, and the youngest, or bongsu, was Mak Su.

After her shower, Anisah was about to slip into her track pants when her mother passed her a sarong° to wear.

"It's very hot today, Anisah," her mother said. "Don't wear your track pants. Put this on."

At the breakfast table, Anisah noticed that all the women were wearing sarongs. Mak Su had decided to join them for breakfast, cradling her baby in her arm. The adult men, according to her mother, had left in the morning, 'to survey some land'. Aidil was playing with a white plastic clip that was used to fix the checkered plastic tablecloth to the edge of the table. He was flicking it first in one direction, and then the other.

"Aidil," said Mak Long, tearing pieces of jemput-jemput into half, steam escaping from their insides. She had naturally heavy eyelids, which gave her either a sleepy, or cynical expression. "You flick that thing one more time and I will flick your balls."

Anisah turned to her mother, wide-eyed. But her mother did not look alarmed at all.

"So how come Anisah decided to come this time?" Mak Su asked Anisah's mother.

"She usually stays at her grandmother's," she replied, referring to her own mother-in-law. "But we decided that this year she's old enough to come along for the drive."

"She's started primary school, right?"

"Of course," said Anisah's mother. "She's in Primary Four already."

Mak Su's baby started to cry. Without any hesitation, Mak Su unbuttoned her blouse to feed him. Anisah's mother could see that her daughter was stunned.

"Do you have to do that here?" she asked.

"He also needs his breakfast," Mak Su replied.

"In front of Aidil?" Anisah's mother said, although she had meant to say 'in front of Anisah'.

"Aidil's still a kid. Right, Aidil? He's not even circumcised yet. When are you going to get circumcised, Aidil?"

Aidil said, "I don't know."

"You better do it soon," Mak Su said. "The older you get, the tougher the foreskin becomes. Then they will have to do it with an axe."

Aidil flinched in his seat. "Mak Su is just trying to scare me," he said.

"I know a boy once," said Mak Long. "He was twelve when he finally got circumcised. They had to use a saw. It took three days and three nights to finally get it off."

"I don't believe you," said Aidil. But Anisah could see that he was nervous. She looked at Mak Su, cooing at her baby, strands of hair falling over her face. Mak Su was the fairest of the three sisters. She could see the faint veins on Mak Su's breast.

"Don't stare at Mak Su like that, Anisah," her mother said.

"Anisah," said Mak Long. "You look like you want some. If you ask Mak Su, I'm sure she'll let you have the other one."

Anisah could feel the rush of blood to her ears. She had

never heard adults speak like this in front of her before. She didn't know whether to feel embarrassed, or thrilled. She regretted not following her parents earlier, on their trips to 'see relatives in Selangor'. But the name of the state itself sounded boring, a sound one might make while yawning. If only she had known!

Over the next few days, Anisah took every opportunity to stick close to her mother when the women gathered to talk. At times, she was confused by some of their references; they talked about mortars and pestles, about sewing machine needles, about umbrellas and raincoats. She wanted to learn this language one day; there was something deeply illicit about it, of words slyly wrapped within words.

But most of the time, what Anisah enjoyed most was the fearless music of their laughter. One night, she lost the thread of the conversation and fell asleep on her mother's lap.

"Wake up," her mother called. "We've arrived."

Anisah rubbed her eyes. They were at the immigration checkpoint. The customs officer was flipping through their passports. He peered into the back seat of the car and knitted his brow. When he returned the stack of passports, he said, "You should change your daughter's photo. She looks different now."

"It's your hair," Anisah's father said. "It's grown longer."

"It's not just her hair," her mother said. Anisah straightened up in her seat and tried to catch her mother's reflection in the rear-view mirror. But her mother was looking straight ahead, as if to return her look was to ruin a mystery that she had passed to Anisah to unwrap, in her own time.

Paya Lebar, 5 AM

His mother wakes him up. He finds his way to the kitchen, then the toilet, and then performs ablutions for the Subuh° prayers. He doesn't like to pray with the lights on; probably he has noticed that everything feels closer in the dark, including God. Maybe Paradise is also a place of darkness, the difference being that the Chosen Ones will be able to see.

After the ritual prayer, he sits to perform the doa, the personal entreaty. He can't think of anything particular— the exams are still months away, no medical crisis in the family—so he opts for the usual: protect us from temptation and harm. His hands are cupped, at the level of his chest. In the dark too, perhaps, God's blessings are received like a spider-filament of light, pouring into the concavity of his palms, visible only to the unseen angels.

Village Radio

When I first entered Pok° Su's house the first thing I noticed was an ornate bird cage, hung near a window. There was a spotted dove cooing inside. Another bird cage hung next to it, but it was empty. I asked Pok Su how he managed to catch the bird.

"From the jungle," was his terse reply.

I wanted him to elaborate. Did he set a trap, and could I see one?

Pok Su looked at me incredulously. "All you have to do is open the cage door, and one will fly in."

It was my turn to be incredulous. Did he perhaps lay some bait inside the cage?

Pok Su turned his attention to the dove, making clucking noises at it. I was getting quite tired with his mystifications. This was what was considered the 'wisdom' of village people, and I began to see that it was built on secrecy and evasion.

Exasperated at not getting straight answers, I asked Pok Su, "Don't you think that it's wrong to keep birds like that? Shouldn't they be allowed to fly freely?"

Pok Su turned towards me. He smiled and said, "You come from the city, where you have radios to keep you company. But I have this dear bird to fill my house with music."

I thought there was something unfortunate about having to imprison an animal merely for entertainment, but I held my tongue. Anyway, he had already drawn a line, putting me in my place. What did I know, as a 'city person', about how these village-dwellers furnish their solitude?

A few months lapsed before I returned to Terengganu. This time, both cages in Pok Su's house were empty. I asked him what happened to the dove. Pok Su merely smiled and brought me to the kitchen. He showed me his brand new transistor radio. Then his wife served us some tea with Jacob's cream crackers.

Throughout the six days that I stayed with him, Pok Su never once turned on the radio. He would, instead, sit in the living room, smoking and staring at his two empty cages. His head was itself a cage, in the cage was a jungle, and in the jungle was music, both private, and faraway.

After The Dusk Prayers

After the dusk prayers, Mak Jah would climb down the few steps in front of her first-storey flat with a plastic bag in her hand. She would slip into her brown rubber slippers and make her way to the park, all the while smiling to herself.

At the park, Mak Jah would find a spot on a bench, preferably one that was not directly under a street lamp. She would look around for anyone who might look officious. She had a particular nervousness about those men in short-sleeved shirts and pants, who wore a lanyard around their necks. Attached to it would be a tag, which she imagined being flashed in her face, to demonstrate the person's power over her.

Mak Jah would then untie her plastic bag and take out some sheets of newspaper to lay on the ground. She would then pinch some fish from the bag, placing them on the sheets.

And then she would wait for her friends to arrive.

Before long, a grey tabby appeared, tentative, staring straight at Mak Jah as if sizing her up. Mak Jah made soft, clucking noises to encourage him. He moved closer, the advance of each timid paw calculated as if he was testing the temperature of the ground.

Could he tell she was an old woman who was incapable of chasing him? Does human age secrete its particular smell? The tabby inched forward, and was soon chewing quite contentedly on the fish. Mak Jah bent down to scratch his head, and he started to purr.

"Where are the rest of your friends?" she asked.

Within seconds, other cats appeared, and very soon Mak Jah's feast had accommodated a total of six. Two of them were white, with black patches, and she asked them if they were siblings. One of them, a scrawny brown tabby, was especially vocal, and would stop in the middle of nosing around the food to arch its head upwards and meow at Mak Jah. She imagined that he was complaining, "Nenek°, they're not letting me have my share!"

She lifted him (she found out it was a her) onto her own lap, reached into her plastic bag, and fed her with her own hand. "Why is this special one so pampered?" she asked. She knew all Malay grandmothers had the same habit: to chide the grandchildren even as they were extravagantly indulging them.

Mak Jah thought about her time in the kampung°. She had kept chickens then, and every morning she would scatter grains of rice in the compound outside the house. There was also a cat called Comot, who was such a needy, hyperactive nuisance, whose favourite mode of getting attention was by weaving his body between one's legs while one was walking. The men all swore at him, but the women, who walked around in long sarongs, had no problems with him.

Comot's favourite spot was under a hibiscus bush outside their house. Mak Jah wondered what had happened to him. Sometimes, she also wondered if this practice of feeding the neighbourhood cats was a kind of penance for not having brought him along when they all moved. The whole family searched the kampung for him, but he was not to be found. Comot liked chasing butterflies...

When Mak Jah arrived home, her son was waiting for her. He said, "Mak, you can't leave the door unlocked when you leave the house. How many times do we have to remind you? We're not living in the kampung anymore, you know."

"I forgot," said Mak Jah, brushing past him into the kitchen to wash her hands.

"And have you seen today's newspapers?"

Overnight

For her son's ninth birthday, Farisha decided to buy him a tent. Her father had lived on Pulau Ubin, and her earliest memories were of the sea. On a breezy Saturday, the family of three assembled a blue trapezoid structure at Changi Beach.

"Is this our new house?" asked Ihsan.

Farisha's husband said, "Yah. Do you like it?"

"It's nice," said Ihsan. "But it's too small."

Farisha said, "We'll stay overnight here. It's going to be very cosy inside."

The spot they had picked was located along a row of eleven other tents. Farisha unpacked a few packets of nasi lemak° and they started to eat. After their lunch Farisha's husband took Ihsan fishing. Farisha stayed back to look after the tent, and before long she found herself chatting with a couple of women.

One of them used to have a relative on Pulau Ubin, a man who conducted Quran classes. Farisha laughed as she recalled a rhyme they used to chant, secretly and with mischievous relish: 'Alif Ba Ta, Pak Haji mata buta, nak cium anak dara, tercium bontot kuda'—'The Quran teacher is blind, he wants to kiss the girl, but he ends up kissing the horse's behind'.

They talked about their childhoods in their respective

kampungs. This was something Farisha could never share with her husband, as he was a Queenstown estate boy for most of his life. They talked about being woken up by roosters, the rain clattering on zinc roofs, nights scented by the haze from mosquito coils.

"The government took away our kampung," Farisha said, "and they gave us camping!"

By night time, Farisha was acquainted with all the families in her makeshift neighbourhood. Her husband had brought back chicken wings, sausages and fishballs. (To compensate for the fact that he did not manage to catch any fish, Farisha thought.) When she saw him lugging the bags of food back to the tent, she teased him good-naturedly: "Someone just got promoted is it? Are you now Station Inspector?"

Her husband was bashful. "We share-share lah tonight. Who knows when we'll see these people again."

During the barbecue, Farisha's husband borrowed a guitar from someone and serenaded Farisha with Sweet Charity's 'Kamelia'. A couple of others joined in the chorus, miming air guitar and clapping beats on their laps. Ihsan had made friends with some of the other children and unveiled to his parents the result of their seashell-hunting expedition.

Before sleeping, Ihsan said to his father, "I didn't know you could play the guitar. Can you teach me one day?" His father promised to buy him one if he did well for his exams. Farisha was the first to drift to sleep, the sound of the waves a familiar, regretful lullaby.

The next morning, Farisha was woken up by a commotion at the tent next door. When she peeked out of her tent, a Park Ranger approached her and demanded that she show him her camping permit. While dutifully searching through her handbag, she overheard someone shout, "I don't want to see your face here again, you understand or not?" Another woman was pleading, "We have nowhere else to go. HDB° took back our flat."

There was something familiar about the proceedings, but Farisha concentrated on locating her permit. She handed it to the Park Ranger, who reminded her to vacate by noon. Farisha realised that no reminiscence of the kampung was complete without the memory of eviction: a rooster crowing at dusk, a roof collapsing under rain, and the ember of a mosquito coil fading from orange, to grey, to a delicate pellet of dust.

Geylang Serai, 6 AM

With a knife, she cuts open the plastic bag of noodles and empties it into a tray. She looks at the hardened, yellow block in front of her, almost overwhelmed by the desire to sculpt it: thumbs for the eye sockets, knuckles for the mouth. Instead, she slips her fingers between the matted strands, feeling the once-impregnable, once-compact labyrinth thaw into slithery, doughy jumbles of string.

Her father's back is turned, sweating from the task of chopping chillies. She closes her eyes, relishing the transgression against the stern, remembered warning: don't play with other people's food.

A *Hantu Tetek* Story

As she held the X-rays in her hand, Sarimah remembered the story of the Hantu Tetek, the buxom ghost who prowled at dusk and killed children by placing their heads between her breasts. What a way to perish, nose squashed against sternum, ears walled in by hot, yeasty flesh. Snuffed out like a candle between forefinger and thumb, death spelt with a pair of double Ds. Her mind turned towards forensic speculation: what was the nature of the death, how long did one struggle in the darkness before being plunged into a deeper oblivion?

She had once read a newspaper article about an American who suffered a concussion after his head was smacked by the knockers of a lap-dancer; subsequently he had sued her for damages. Maybe this was the case with the Hantu Tetek. Pectoral boulders which it used to crush delinquent skulls, those truants still playing hide-and-seek even after the twilight prayer call—to adults a summons, to children a warning—had long exhaled its final notes.

Sarimah considered how it was the morphology of the breasts which ultimately decided the mode of homicide. Maybe there was no tissue in them at all—they were pure muscle, reptilian, flecked with fungal patches of scales, and they could constrict a child's head, squeezing the carotids like grapes. The Hantu's nipples seeking out one another, to be united in an auto-erotic serpent's kiss. If not muscular, then cystic, globes stretched thin by gallons of fluid, streaked with veins like river charts on a map. Asphyxiation, all the victim's pores buttered up, nostrils plugged by slug-like extensions, blobs of gelatine.

Or perhaps a more profound death, a mystery hidden in the cleavage of the Hantu Tetek, a red glow, porthole portal, a landscape from the point of view of an embryo, promising eternal warmth, deliverance from a night filled with the chilly shouts of parents and a guaranteed spanking at home. Unlike the boys in her kampung, Sarimah did not believe the power of the Hantu Tetek was in her overt carnality—unlike the Pontianak, the soft-spoken, tombstone-cradling seductress who exuded sex from her hair and frangipani from her pores. Hantu Tetek practised no gender discrimination; boys and girls were equal prey, as long as they had strayed beyond the magic circle bounded by the front yard and the clock's hands.

Moreover, didn't her mother tell Sarimah that the Hantu Tetek's breasts were monstrosities—putrid hives of maggots? A paradox then, a mortal ghost, with breasts that kept on rotting, but never towards complete disintegration. This then was the Hantu Tetek's torment and the source of her malevolence: that the only organs on her body showing signs of life were the ones that were undergoing eternal putrefaction. Cells budding only to decay the next second, it was anybody's idea of Hell: to be revived and then tortured, resurrected and put through unimaginable pain. To be alive means to be dying—it was a fact that Sarimah was getting used to, a universal truth she had to acknowledge. Especially now.

Sarimah held an X-ray, or more specifically, a mammogram,

against the window. Those radiolucent patches, what the doctors called 'calcifications', became brighter, inflamed. With almost a cry of dismay Sarimah scanned the phantom-like patches. She held her mammogram higher towards the light. She saw ghosts, brazen and invincible, immune to the powers of sunlight and prayer.

Cold Comfort

As Razmi slipped into his lab coat, what struck him was the ease of his transformation. He had entered the hospital in a long-sleeved shirt and pants, like any other visitor. Now, by slinging his stethoscope across his neck, he assumed an authority which he often felt disproportionate to his age. What right was his to ask these patients the most intrusive questions, to demand their trust, to suggest to them, his face guileless, his eyes blinking, that to withhold from him the knowledge of their bodies was to deprive him of an education?

Razmi sighed. His patients were his teachers. But how strange the relationship—it was the student who prepared the classroom by drawing the U-shaped curtain around the bed, the one who ended up examining the teacher. No, Razmi thought, his patients were not so much his teachers, as his textbooks.

"There's a case at Bed 26," his coursemate told him. "Nulliparous, with breech presentation. She's got an interesting history."

His coursemate's name was Cheryl, a chirpy, bespectacled girl, with a habit of nodding vigorously when a senior registrar led them on ward rounds. Razmi did not know much about her, except for the fact that both her parents were doctors.

Sometimes he felt a certain envy at what he imagined

to be her dinner table conversations; her parents dropping names of their colleagues, Cheryl's eyes lighting up in recognition and awe, her pride at being enrolled into elite tradition. Razmi's own parents were educated only up to secondary school level. Sometimes, stealing a look at Cheryl's unaccountably fresh morning-lesson countenance, he wondered which burden of expectation was heavier: to be like one's parents, or to surpass them.

"You've examined her already?" Razmi asked.

"Yah. But I think she'll give you a better history. Her English isn't very good."

The patient at Bed 26 turned out to be a Malay girl, barely out of her teens. She had very dark, dry lips, which Razmi automatically assumed to be caused by heavy smoking. Her eyebrows had been plucked very thinly, and her hair was dyed brown, with black roots showing. When Razmi first saw her, she was staring blankly into space, a blanket drawn over her abdomen. He had speculated that she was doing so not because she was cold, but because of habit—even at such a late stage she was still self-conscious of her pregnancy.

"Hi," Razmi said. "I'm a medical student. Can I ask you a few questions?"

The girl looked at Razmi warily. "Just now got one girl ask me already."

"Yah, I know," Razmi replied. "If you're tired it's all right." He felt somehow relieved, and eager to retreat to the conference room, where he had placed his bag, his notes, his real textbooks, filled with illustrations and remote photographs of Caucasian case studies, their eyes discreetly masked. He suddenly felt annoyed at Cheryl for referring this particular patient to him, as if she was trying to make a point. But what point exactly?

"You're Malay right?" the girl suddenly asked him. She then said in Malay, "You can speak Malay, right?"

Razmi nodded. He was used to interviewing Malay patients, and very often these encounters involved them confiding something in him, which went beyond whatever intimate knowledge he had gathered about bowel habits or abnormal discharges. He was drawn into a compact, established by a shared language, which guaranteed something different from mere rapport. It felt closer but also stickier. He could only surmise that it felt like some kind of kinship. Since these patients were mostly older than him, he was for that moment on loan, an adopted son, an able-bodied ferryman of hopes.

"During my time, there were not many Malay doctors. It's good to see our people progressing."

"You know these nurses from China, they don't understand English at all. Like that can become nurse?"

"Your parents must be so proud of you. Sejuk perut mak mengandung."

That last remark always made him smile. It literally meant that his mother's womb was 'cold' when she was carrying him. It was supposed to refer to how the pregnancy was a blessed one. And yet nothing he had studied indicated how uterine temperature had anything to do with a child's intelligence or temperament.

"So this is your first?" he asked the girl, in Malay.

"Yah," the girl replied. "I can't wait to give birth. I haven't touched a cigarette in nine months. So what do you want to ask me?"

Over the next few minutes Razmi solicited her history. There was a checklist in his notebook, which he went through methodically. Apparently the girl had been informed that there was a possibility of a forceps delivery.

"He kicks so hard," she said. "I think he kicked around so much until he's now upside down. You know where he got that from? His father's a football player."

"Professional player?" Razmi asked. "What's his name?"

"I don't want to mention his name. Don't want to shame him. He's got his own career, his own life. Now he's got another girlfriend already."

Razmi had given the girl the benefit of the doubt. But here she was revealing herself as yet another unsavoury statistic: the unwed teenage mother from the problem minority. Was it because of people like her that Razmi chose to study medicine? He wondered whether the girl had told Cheryl that her pregnancy was unplanned. He felt angry all of a sudden, as if she had undone all the work he had put in to cultivate an image agreeable under the gaze of those like Cheryl.

"You got girlfriend?" she asked Razmi.

Was this some kind of flirtation? Razmi spoke without looking at her. "No." And then he raised his face to square against hers, surprised at how irritated, even sarcastic, he sounded. "I think I'm still too young to get into a relationship. There are more important things in life. I want to think carefully about my future."

The girl seemed to sense Razmi's prickliness. "I'm not trying to tackle you," she said. "You're going to be a doctor. Guys like you don't look at girls like me. They usually go for Chinese girls. I'm just asking only. Anyway what's your name?"

Razmi cleared his throat. "Razmi," he said, in a small voice.

"It's a nice name. What does it mean?"

"I'm not sure."

"Maybe I'll name my baby 'Razmi'. Then when he grows up he'll also become a doctor."

Razmi did not know what to say. He wanted to share with the girl that his parents were fans of a Malay singer, called R. Azmi, but he was afraid she would recognise the name, bog him in conversation. He saw Cheryl enter the ward, smiling, looking congenial and authoritative at the same time.

"So sorry you're having so many interviews today," she said to the girl. "Are you guys done? I'm thinking of grabbing lunch."

"Ya," Razmi said. "We've finished."

Cheryl turned to the girl and affected a look of concern. "We better let you rest. Are you still feeling cold?"

The girl smiled. "A bit. But not my legs. More my stomach." She looked at Razmi and jokingly said, "Sejuk perut". A final adhesive, flimsy, worth a laugh, before Razmi peeled himself away from her world and rejoined his own, to discuss the complications of her pregnancy with Cheryl at the air-conditioned cafeteria downstairs.

Sacrifice

Suhaili was smoking by her bedroom window. It had been three days since she came back from prison, and she had so far resisted lighting up at home. But she had to make the bedroom her own again—her sister had been occupying it for the past year—and the only way to do that was to leave the smell of smoke in the curtains, the bedsheets, her pillow.

Everything in her bedroom was the same, and the only trace of her sister's residence was a poster of a Korean star she had forgotten to remove from the inside of the wardrobe door. When Suhaili first saw the poster, she was reminded of her own absence—the fact that she was not around to see her sister become a teenager.

Actually, there was another trace her sister had left behind. The bottle of perfume that Jasper had bought for Suhaili was half empty. Suhaili recalled that he had given it to her as a birthday present, just a few days before her arrest. It must have taken some restraint for Suhaili's sister to use only half the bottle in the space of a year. Or Suhaili's mother might have told her, "You can't use that, that perfume is Suhaili's." She was comforted by this thought. It meant that a part of her had always been at home.

Jasper had not written to her when she was in prison. She remembered the first few letters she sent him. Inmates were provided with a single sheet of paper, whose edges could be folded in and stuck together to form an envelope. How she had tried to squeeze in as many words as possible, reducing the spaces between them, her handwriting suddenly spidery and emaciated. The final letter she wrote to him consisted of nine words: 'Jasper, my love, please write back. Your baby Elly.' She wrote them in giant letters, which gave her a kind of release. No more for her those stunted, spring-coiled words.

It was Jasper who introduced her to Ice. He had first taken it discreetly, spending a long time in the toilet, but it did not take long for him to start smoking in front of her. She tried to make him quit, and broke his meth pipe on a few occasions, but he always found a way to get new ones. One day, Suhaili asked for a taste. Jasper resisted at first, but was soon teaching her the proper way to inhale.

Suhaili had a plan in mind. She would try the Ice with him, but would prove to him that it would be possible to quit. All it took was willpower. Suhaili prided herself on her discipline. She was working as a waitress, but still managed her time well enough to enrol in a hairdressing course.

A month later, Suhaili's strategy became more modest. She would instead help to 'pace' him. They would ration out their Ice sessions—once in the morning, and another after dinner. And then they started to take it about three times a day, then five, and by that time Suhaili had quit her job, her school, and had moved in with him.

She had also become acquainted with his dealer, and on the day of the arrest had met him to replenish their weekly supply. As it turned out, she was caught in a sting operation, and her urine tested positive for Ice and Ecstasy. She claimed to the investigating officers that the drugs that she was about to procure were for 'personal use'. She made the dealer promise that he would not mention Jasper's name to the police.

Suhaili finished her cigarette. She remembered the first time she met Jasper at the Italian restaurant, and his first words to her.

"Do you believe in angels?" he asked her.

"Why?"

"I don't believe in them, because I'm not really religious. But I see one now clearing my table."

On hindsight, she knew it was the drugs talking. Nevertheless, the memory left her with a pang in her chest. The day before, she had visited Jasper's walk-up apartment, only to find out that it had been rented to an expat couple. They had never heard of Jasper. Suhaili wondered, as she had countless times in prison, whether Jasper himself had been arrested, had overdosed, or had committed suicide.

She would not know that Jasper was now living in London. Her arrest was a sign for him to put his life in order. After he heard that she had gone in, he joined his parents in the UK and checked himself into rehab. He found a job as head of marketing in his father's company. He found religion. He thought of Suhaili sometimes, as an example of God's saving grace. He would tell some of his faithless colleagues: "At your hour of need, God will send down an angel to turn your life around. Such is His love for His poor creatures."

Tampines, 7 AM

They've taken a spot near the MRT° doors, and their tans reveal that they have returned from a camping expedition, rather than heading for one. They are surrounded by oversized backpacks and a portable hi-fi set, which one of them insisted on calling a 'mini compo', to the amusement of the rest. This same figure is now observing one of the girls leave through the train doors, staring intently at her bag, or more specifically, its front pocket, into which he had slipped in a note.

The night before, he had sat beside the girl by the campfire, while the rest were asleep, and he had pointed at stars and furnished pauses with a sigh and the phrase, "It's nice ah, like this?" If only there was some way to tell if she would read his message, but one thing was certain: already the waves have begun to erase the charred remains of whatever had lent them those orange and haloed masks for the night.

Give Me a Simple One

Hamidah's handphone rang while she was on the bus. Startled, she started rummaging through her bag, not so much to answer it but to kill the noise that it was making. She did not like the sound of her ringtone. It was a sound one would associate with young people, with its cheerful and modern beat. Her daughter had chosen it for her while fiddling with it one day.

It was her daughter on the line. She was sobbing.

"Mak," she said, "What am I going to do?"

"Why are you crying? What happened?" Hamidah asked.

"I haven't had my period for a while now."

"Are you sick? If you are I'll bring you to see the doctor."

Her daughter said she wasn't sick. Hamidah knew this too.

"Wait for me," Hamidah said. "I'll be home in a while."

Hamidah later found out that her daughter had been seeing a Chinese boy from her polytechnic. They had been together for half a year.

"Does he want to marry you?" Hamidah asked.

Her daughter shook her head.

"It's a big sin," Hamidah said. "A terrible sin."

"I know, Mak," the girl started moaning. "I did such a shameful thing."

"No," Hamidah said. "It's a sin to get rid of it. I hope he's not asking you to do it."

The next morning, Hamidah sat down with her daughter. She had kept her promise not to tell her husband for the time being. She told her daughter of her plan.

"You should have the baby. And if your boyfriend doesn't want to marry you, I will adopt it."

"What do you mean, adopt it?"

"I will raise him like my own son."

The girl looked puzzled.

"You still haven't finished school," Hamidah continued. "You can't raise a child on your own. If I adopt him, then you can treat him as if he's your little brother."

Hamidah knew that what she was saying made little sense to the girl. Can her daughter live with her own child as if he were a sibling? But Hamidah had been struck by a thought while lying in bed the night before. She, her husband, and her daughter were all dark-skinned. (She also wondered what the boy saw in her daughter, and for a brief moment felt strangely proud of the mystery of her daughter's attractiveness.)

This new offspring, however, could take after his father. He could be made to swallow the lie that he had been handed to them one day, in a bundle, by a Chinese family. If he believed it, Hamidah's family would one day believe it too. He would be fed with formula milk from day one; Hamidah would not allow him to be breastfed.

Her daughter nodded slowly, with a faraway look in her eyes, as if the shadow of her future was being cast over her face. During the next few days, she weighed Hamidah's plan in her mind, picturing Hamidah with the baby on her lap...at the balcony, in the living room, at the dining table, under the glow of the pendant lamp.

One week later, she had an abortion performed.

"I can't give it to you, Mak," she told Hamidah.

Hamidah stared at the sofa that her daughter was sitting on. She could not look her daughter in the eye.

"I want to give you a grandchild."

Hamidah did not hear what her daughter was saying. She was recalling another time, not too long ago, when her daughter was lying on the sofa, holding up a handphone. She had just bought it for Hamidah as a birthday present, and was choosing a ringtone for her.

"Is this one nice?" she asked. "It sounds very classic."

"Anything."

Her daughter rolled her eyes. "Mak, it's your phone, you have to choose."

"Just give me a simple one."

"Mak," her daughter laughed, her eyes lit by the handphone screen. "There is no simple one."

The Morning Ride

Two months after Amin had started secondary school, his father asked him, "Do you know of anyone called 'Kevin' in your school?"

"No," said Amin. "Why?"

"He's my boss' son."

Amin considered this fact for a moment. "What does he look like?"

"Tall boy," his father replied, chewing thoughtfully, as if there was a fine fish bone mixed up with the rice in his mouth, "with spectacles."

Every weekday morning, Amin's father would wake up and dress in a short-sleeved shirt and pants which Amin's mother had ironed the night before. When Amin woke up, his father would already be dressed, at the kitchen table, with his favourite beige ceramic mug (although Amin could not imagine his father having a favourite anything; the mug was just an exclusive object that was part of his authority). When Amin finished showering, his father would already have left the house, the aroma of strong black coffee suspended in the cool air of the kitchen.

Amin wondered why his father took so long to tell him about Kevin. He had not dared to ask whether Kevin was the person whom the father sent to his school every morning.

Because of the way his father had avoided looking at him, Amin knew this must be so.

He remembered filling up a form when he was in primary school, where he was supposed to list his parents' occupations. For his father, he had written down 'chauffeur'. Proudly, he showed his father the form, expecting some praise, especially since he believed that 'chauffeur' sounded foreign, and was a difficult word to spell. But his father had made him write 'driver' instead.

"But driver can be anything, right, Ayah°?" Amin asked. "Can be taxi driver, or lorry driver?"

"Never mind," the father said. "They don't need to know what kind of driver your father is."

Amin had sensed at that time that there were aspects of his father's life meant to be hidden from others, and maybe from Amin as well. Once, his mother had pointed out to Amin the car that his father drove. On that day, his father had forgotten to bring his handphone along with him, and had to retrieve it from home. The car was a large, black Mercedes-Benz, conspicuous among the smaller cars and motorcycles in the car park. When his father got out of the car, he looked around nervously, before his eyes settled on the windows of his own house. Amin's mother had pulled him aside and told him, "Don't let your father know."

Then there was another time when he overheard his parents quarrelling in their bedroom. Apparently his father had threatened to quit his job. It had to do with his employer's wife referring to him to her friends as 'my Ahmad', even though 'Ahmad' was not his name. In the middle of the argument, his father had warned his mother not to raise her voice, in case Amin could hear them.

The day after he learnt about Kevin, Amin woke up feeling as if he had not had enough sleep. He could hear the sound of his father making coffee, the clink of his teaspoon, like a morning bell, against the cup. When Amin entered the kitchen, he suddenly felt a pinprick of jealousy and almost asked his father, "Are you going to send Kevin to school?" But he knew that his voice would come out wrong—too high, or too accusing—so he padded purposefully into the toilet, latching the aluminium door in relief.

On the bus ride to school, Amin thought about the journey his father was making. His father would take a bus to his employer's house. Upon arriving, he would start the engine of the black Mercedes. And then a boy, wearing the same school uniform as Amin, would enter the car. Most probably, the boy would sit at the back, beside his schoolbag. Had his father ever told the boy about Amin's existence? And did the boy then suggest, without giving it much thought, that the father could ask Amin along, so he could have company on the car ride to school?

Amin looked in front of him, at the backs of the heads of other passengers in the bus. He closed his eyes and tried to imagine a scenario in the black Mercedes. Where would Amin sit in the car? Out of respect to his father, he would of course sit in the front passenger seat. But that would mean he was somewhat apart from his fellow schoolmate at the back. But if he were to sit at the back, he would leave his father alone in front, a man reduced from a father to a chauffeur, just as his own presence was reduced to a pair of furtive eyes in the rear-view mirror.

It was just as well that his father did not tell Kevin about him. But why then did his father tell Amin about Kevin? By doing so, he had exposed a part of his life which he had previously maintained behind a wall of discretion. Amin wondered if his father's act had been a kind of warning, or a plea. His father had dropped out at the end of his primary school studies, because of the sudden death of his own father, a man who used to groom horses at the Bukit Timah Saddle Club. Now Amin had superseded his father, and had become, by virtue of his education alone, the equal of someone whom his father served and ferried.

Amin thought about the tall, bespectacled boys that he had seen in school. Which one of them could be Kevin? He saw himself in his father's place, at the wheel. There would always be a Kevin looking over his shoulder. And Amin's job was to study hard, to maintain a lead, where being in front was not a matter of indignity, but triumph. Only by overtaking his father, Amin thought, would he be able to get close to the source of his father's secret pride.

Shallow Focus

It was my mother's idea to take our family portrait in a professional studio. I had just had my convocation and she insisted that I pose for the photograph in my blue rented robe.

"When did we become a Chinese family?" I asked. "Only Chinese people do this kind of thing."

"That's because they send their children to university," my mother snapped. "Anyway, which mother wouldn't be proud that her son is a graduate?"

Actually, the reason I was making a fuss was because I was worried for my sister. She was in her final year at an arts college, and it was unlikely that she would enter a university. I didn't think she would appreciate a reminder of this immortalised in a blown-up portrait.

My sister, however, appeared nonchalant about the whole affair. The day before the shoot, she asked my mother for some money so that she could 'do her hair'. This inspired my mother to also pay a visit to the hair salon. I also thought I could do with a haircut, until I realised that there was no point to it. I was going to be wearing that ridiculous mortarboard on my head.

My father was the one who had made the booking, at a studio near our house in Bishan. When we arrived, a surly woman, perched on a glass-top counter, asked us to wait. A few minutes later, the photographer appeared from behind a black velvet curtain. I scanned his face and asked, "Min Heng?"

Min Heng was a secondary school classmate, and my fiercest academic rival. I remembered the time in Secondary Three, when I had slipped to second position in class, behind him. My mother cancelled our holiday plans to Australia and engaged a tuition teacher for my weakest subject, Geography. The next year I topped the class.

"Wah, long time, man," Min Heng said.

"Yah," I said. We had lost touch after we went to separate junior colleges. "This is your studio?"

"No lah," he said. "I'm doing this freelance. Trying to raise some money for my exhibition."

We were ushered to a studio, and I changed into my academic dress behind a screen. After I was done I observed Min Heng instructing my parents to sit on two wooden armchairs. There was a screen behind them, a giant, maroon sheet of paper that had been unrolled from a horizontal spool.

"Your gold and white hood," Min Heng said. "That's Engineering, right?"

"Yah," I said. For some reason I was beginning to feel embarrassed. What I had expected to be merely vulgar was turning out to be insensitive as well.

After the family portrait, Min Heng asked if I wanted to have an individual shot, against a different backdrop.

"I'll throw it in for free," he said. "Old friends what."

"Why not? Since we're here," my mother replied, beaming.

The backdrop that Min Heng referred to was a painted bookshelf. I was made to pose beside a dark wooden desk, with a miniature desktop globe placed on it. Min Heng seemed oblivious to my discomfort. As we were about to leave, Min Heng passed me his name card.

"If you got any friends who want to take photos, call me lah," he said. "Can give them good rates."

I was silent during our drive back home. As we were reaching the car park, my mother said, "You remember how I always told you to become like him?"

"Yes," I said. "Always follow whatever the Chinese students do. Find out what's their secret."

My mother smiled. "Now he's asking you to help him find work."

"So what, Mak?" I raised my voice. "Does that mean I've become more Chinese than him?"

In the evening, I went to my sister's room after a very tense dinner. My mother had refused to speak to me after my outburst. I gazed at my sister's school project, a stack of photographs she had laid out on her table.

"What a silly thing to say," she said. "So he's doing what makes him happy. Does that mean he's become more Malay than you?"

"What makes you think I'm not happy doing Engineering?"

"I don't know," she said. "Are you?"

I didn't answer her question. Instead, I looked at the images that she had taken. They were dreamy close-ups of flowers, the light illuminating and exposing the veins on their translucent petals.

Telok Blangah, 8 AM

She sits at the table, marking her students' books, and suddenly hears some giggling at the back of the class. She glares at the source of the noise and asks rhetorically, "Do you write your composition with your hands or your mouth?" And then, in case the sarcasm was missed, "No words." But the reign of silence is an impossible dream.

Thinking is a noisy activity, and she soon devises a mental inventory of the various sounds which constitute the otherwise quotidian hum of the classroom. There is head-scratching, pencil-tapping, chair-rocking, shoes striking table legs, hands rustling through pages, and from a far corner, the increasingly agitated sighs of a girl, finally reaching an orchestral crescendo when she puts up her hand and asks, without waiting to be called, "Cikgu°, what if it's less than 500 words? I don't know what to write anymore!"

Litter Girl

My name was on the board. For two weeks I was assigned plainclothes duty, to nab those who littered in public. My colleagues told me that the National Environment Agency was recruiting younger members from the auxiliary police force not just because they were shorthanded. Apparently, people had started to wise up to their tactics. A typical profile of one of their enforcement officers was a middle-aged man, who liked reading The New Paper while hanging around groups of youths. The size of the tabloid made it convenient for him to keep a lookout while pretending to read.

My designated spot was near a bus interchange, where there were seats carved into a circular brick structure. On my first three days, I managed to catch an average of eight offenders a day. On my fourth day, it rained. I saw some people lighting up but they were moving as they smoked, following the path along the covered walkway.

I was tempted to tail some of them, counting down to the moment when ash would touch the filter, the decisive moment when someone would commit an unthinking crime. But it made my job more sneaky than what I was comfortable with. If I were to position myself at the seats, watching from the side of my eye, then I was more a witness than a spy.

The skies only cleared when it was almost evening. My usual seat was wet. But some people still hung around the brick structure, as if it was not just a resting spot but also a landmark and meeting-point. It struck me that my observations were possible because I was an outsider. It was as if I had an aerial view of the place.

My hopes were raised when a delinquent-looking youth started on a cigarette. However, when he finished, he produced, from his pocket, what looked like a purse. I recognised it as a portable ashtray. It was a kind of anti-climax not to see the cigarette butt flicked, somersaulting into the air, with a contempt I associated with manliness.

I then heard a cigarette lighter flick (I had become sensitive to this sound), and turned to see a young lady inhaling from her stick. She reminded me of the sister of a classmate I once had. His house was often chosen as the venue for group project work, for obvious reasons. Once, I had found his sister's bra, a lacy, black, sinful thing, draped on a wall bracket in the toilet. I told the rest of my group mates, and we all took turns visiting the toilet. Not much work was done, as we accused each other of sniffing the bra, with each of us taking turns confessing, and then retracting. We were passing and shifting the truth among us back and forth as if it was the bra itself, balled up and scorching.

I had almost wished that the young lady would also produce her own portable ashtray, but she let her cigarette butt drop from her fingers onto the pavement. I waited for her to walk away, and then I caught up with her.

"I'm so sorry," she said. "I'm in a rush." It sounded less like an excuse than a sincere apology. She had large eyes, framed by thick, even eyelashes. I felt that I could not look at her eyes for very long for fear of looking into them. I took out my authorisation card from the agency and showed it to her.

The young lady sighed. Somehow I had expected her to

inspect my card, to verify my identity. But it seemed to her that I had already issued her a summons, like a referee who had just flashed her a red card.

"You were smoking over there, just now, right?"

She brushed a few strands of hair with her fingers and tucked them behind her left ear. I have seen girls do this when they are nervous. I wondered what the back of her ears smelt like.

"I don't know," she said. "What proof do you have?"

"The proof is I saw you." I said. "Come with me." I led her to the spot where she had dumped her cigarette butt. Apparently she had shifted it with her shoe to the bank of the pavement, where other cigarette butts lay.

"There's so many there. You can't tell which one is mine."

Fortunately for me, there was a single butt with a lipstick stain on it. I held it up and said, "I think you know where this colour came from. You still want to argue?"

I did not know why I sounded so brash. Where did I pick up such language from?

"Can I have your I/C° please?" I then asked, trying to soften my words, or more exactly, trying to show her that I was capable of softness.

"Is it a fine?" she asked. "Because I'm really broke this month. I'm so sorry. I'll just take that and throw it away. How much is the fine?"

"It's $200. Can I please have your I/C?" I said. My throat was dry.

And then she switched into Malay. "Bang," she said, "can't you give me another chance?"

I had never been in a situation with a beautiful girl like

this before. I had spoken to pretty salesgirls, and waitresses, but I had never been this close. And what I meant by close was that her vulnerability became a form of intimacy. She had used the word 'Bang', short for 'Abang', referring to me as a brother. But the word was also used by wives to call their husbands.

"I promise I won't do it again. Just give me a warning. I promise."

That was not the promise that I wanted from her. I wanted her to promise that I would be able to meet her again, or those like her, without an overblown offence and its ridiculous penalty to make such an encounter possible. I wanted her to promise that women would not just judge me on my physical appearance and allow me to fade into the traffic and scenery of a crowd. I wanted her to promise on their behalf that they would always allow me a second chance.

I took down her name. And her address. I told her that she would receive a letter in two weeks' time. I never kept her details, even though I did not obtain them through underhand methods. I did, however, keep the cigarette butt that she had thrown behind.

Some days, I enter a shopping centre and ask for a match of the shade on the butt. Some salesgirls think that I am doing something romantic. But what interests me more are the fancy names that are given to these shades. Every time I learn a new name, it is as if I have learnt a new thing about her.

Guava Stain. Parisian Pink. All Heart. Strawberry Suede. Craving.

They are like the broken lines to a song, or a poem, whose missing words I will never find.

A Hantu Kumkum Story

Razali was a bodybuilder. Unlike some other body-builders he knew, the body was not so much a lump of clay to be moulded into its ideal shape, but something that was by nature wild and rebellious. Any drop in vigilance, and there would be an adipose uprising—gathering around his abdominal area as a procession of love handles, or demonstrating solidarity by organising a sit-in at his chin area. For Razali, his body was not the product of an artist's dialogue between skill and material, but the subject to a monarch's absolute edicts.

The decision to tame his body was made one day while he was in his secondary school's uniformed group. While practising marching drills, he was humiliated in front of his friends when the drill sergeant barked at him, "I said stomach in, chest out, not the other way round." For the rest of the day, he was sucking in his stomach, only too self-conscious that each time he relaxed, his viscera would push out his abdominal wall, a submarine crew that used his navel as a periscope to view the outside world.

So he found a solution in body fortification. Strips of muscle could be toned to the point where the hidden body would no longer be able to exercise its design plans on the visible one. Flesh could be turned into brace, corset and girdle. He started on a regime of supplements, attended the gym at his community centre four times a week, and within three years became a qualified fitness trainer. He started wearing T-shirts with ripped sleeves (their edges were deliberately jagged to suggest that they had been ripped apart by the force of rampaging biceps), viewed egg yolks and chicken skin with nausea, and got married to a regular patron he would often sign in for free while working as a part-time bouncer at a club.

It was only in the last month or so when Razali started intensifying his workout routines. He had recently joined a new gymnasium located in the city area, and he found himself surrounded by a new batch of veterans who had tuned their bodybuilding pursuits into surgical obsessions. As the mirrors in the gym replicated their tortured grimaces, it also seemed to make their exchanges profuse and repetitious: they talked about nothing else but extra inches to the chest, or the side-effects of creatine monohydrate.

Razali's wife could not help but notice her husband's restlessness. Not without incredulity, she served him banquets, wondering to herself whether the most desperately religious made such offerings to their gods. In bed, he often complained about his colleagues. The giant Zachariah, whose feats at the bench press were just a step away from the miracle of levitation. And how could he even hope to compare his puny self to the twin brothers, Murad and Maidin, who, blessed with the gift of perfect resemblance, could spur themselves through the completely unforced act of sibling rivalry?

After sending her husband off to work one day, Razali's wife opened her refrigerator. Quilts of mist could not hide the obscene largesse she had stocked for her insatiable husband. Suddenly, on the radio, she heard a news report about the Kumkum. The newscaster was trying to quash rumours that the Kumkum had crossed the causeway and was now making its rounds in Singapore, making an appeal to her listeners' sense of rationality and common sense.

The Hantu Kumkum was a ghost who terrorised homes with its hunger for the blood of virgins. She was originally a woman who consulted a bomoh° for a beauty treatment. The bomoh made her consume an elixir, with one condition: that she not look at the mirror for a period of 30 days. However, tormented by curiosity (provoked each time the woman touched the increasingly smooth contours of her face), the woman sneaked a peek at her reflection on the 29th day.

The mirror cracked; and so did the woman's face. She had been scarred by her own impatience. To regain human semblance, she had to feed on the blood of young women, a task that would send her from door to door, draped in a headscarf that masked her abominable countenance. Nobody knows, not even the Kumkum herself, the quota of blood she would have to partake of before complete restoration is possible, which would make her assignment both everlasting, and futile.

A sudden knock on the door brought Razali's wife back to reality, or perhaps yet further into unreality. Superstitiously, she peered into the viewfinder, half-expecting a veiled woman to be brooding at her doorstep. Instead, it was her husband, directing impatient glares at the convex eyehole. Razali's wife noticed how dwarfish he looked, the sides of the corridor like a pair of parentheses that framed him. The only cure for vanity was a curse—their depleted savings, his eroded libido—that would reveal its unappeasable nature. It was not her husband's body that needed repair, but the evil conspiracy of his own eyes.

Proof

Radhiah looked at her watch. Suriati would have finished her shift and would be home by now. She took a deep breath and knocked on the door.

"Assalaamu'alaikum°," she called.

It was one of Suriati's sons who opened the door. He was in Primary Three, and had barely scraped through his final-year exams the year before.

"Mak!" he shouted into the living room. "The ustazah° is here!"

Suriati appeared, wiping her wet hands on the sides of her dress. Radhiah caught a whiff of soap as Suriati opened the padlock to her gate. It was a distinctive smell, belonging to a kind of soap that was cut out from yellow rectangular blocks. Before washing machines came along, it was commonly used for laundry.

As Suriati served her some rose syrup, Radhiah stole a glance at the kitchen. She saw the washing machine and wondered if it was broken.

"How are your boys?" Radhiah asked, taking a sip from her glass. The rose syrup was too sweet for her but she swallowed it calmly.

Suriati turned to look at her sons, who were eating rice with soy sauce and fried eggs in the kitchen.

"They're all right. The younger one stopped wetting his bed," she replied.

"That's good. How did you make him stop?"

Suriati smiled. "I don't know," she said. "One day he just decided to stop. Maybe he's now old enough to feel sorry for his mother."

Radhiah thought it was best to get straight to the point. "You didn't visit your husband the whole of last month. He's been asking for you."

"I've been busy," said Suriati.

"You know that he needs you. He always looks forward to your visits."

Suriati smiled again. "Then what about me? Don't you think I need him too?" Her self-pity was now twisting itself into anger. "When are you going to release him? You keep him for two years, and then you say he's not ready, and you keep him for another two, and another. When does it end?"

"Yati," Radhiah said. "We just have to make sure he doesn't go back to doing..."

"Doing what?" Suriati interrupted. "The first few times you came here you asked me what I thought about Palestine. About Israel. About USA, about Iraq. Do you ask him questions like that too? How can you ask him the same questions for six years?"

"I don't know what they ask him," Radhiah said. "I'm not there at the interviews."

"Then can you tell me what is the right answer? Please tell me. I'll tell him what to say when I see him the next time."

"He can say the right things, but we must make sure that he believes what he's saying."

Suriati stared at Radhiah. She lowered her voice as she spoke.

"How do we know what's in another person's heart?" she asked. "We're not God."

Radhiah felt that their discussion had strayed far from its original purpose. "You'll visit him this month, I hope. He really wants to see you and the boys."

"I can't," Suriati answered. "I can't go on like this. I don't have any education, like you. The best job all of you can find me is as a cleaner."

"Tell us how else we can help you," Radhiah said.

"The boys need a father," Suriati said. "And if it's not him it'll have to be someone else. I'm going to ask for a divorce."

Radhiah spent the next hour trying to convince Suriati to be patient. It's not possible for the government to hold him forever, she insisted. They only did that with the Communists, and her husband wasn't one. It was going to be possible for him to find a job after his release. And then he'd be able to take care of his family once again.

On her way home, Radhiah thought about the report she would have to write. The Rehabilitation Committee would not be pleased to hear that Suriati had decided to move on with her life. The promise of a reunion with his family was one of the things that had made her husband co-operative at the detention centre.

But what if Suriati had made up the whole part about the divorce? Maybe it was her way of exerting some pressure on them to release her husband. Should she mention, in her report, her suspicion that Suriati had not been entirely truthful?

Radhiah realised that doubt was creeping into her heart.

She recognised it as the same feeling that must have seized Suriati's son when he first opened the door, his body half-hidden, his eyes searching Radhiah's face for signs.

Tanjong Pagar, 12 Noon

It's lunch time, and he looks forward to the cigarette that he has been putting off for the past three hours. A practice since his secondary school days—the promise of a reward at the end of an ordeal (discipline and deprivation being close cousins), except that now the carrot is not drawn from a box of biscuits but a small pack of Marlboro Menthol Lights. He fishes in his pockets and realises that he has misplaced his lighter.

With the cigarette hanging from his lips, he takes the elevator down, drops by the Mama Money Changer, only to be told that they have run out of stock. He crosses roads, beats lights, breaks into a run. A man in search of an oasis, his cigarette quivering like a divining rod, not for water but fire.

The Hole

It was a little after I had my lunch when I heard the knock at the door. When I opened it, a polite man greeted me and passed me an envelope. Please collect the body within 24 hours, or it will be buried by the state. There was no room for shock. The whole week I had prepared myself for this. I did not let my hands tremble as I accepted the envelope. I told myself I was receiving something that was weightless.

The man left earlier than I expected. I did not like the idea that he felt it was only proper to leave me to grieve in private. He did not understand that there was no grief. My son and I had not spoken to each other for many years. Unlike his mother, I had refused to visit him in prison. I would have opened the envelope right in front of the man if he had stayed. I would have done it calmly, and when I am done, I will look at him straight in the eyes and say thank you.

But the man would be mistaken if he had thought my actions were calm. Because calmness meant that I was placing my feelings under control. But as I have said, I had no feelings anymore. It was not calmness, but numbness. Very early on I had decided that everything that was happening was a result of fate. It was fate that would hold my son like a puppet from a rope, and it was also fate that would move my hands, also like a puppet, to tear the edge of an envelope.

Inside the envelope was a letter. There was also my son's

pink identity card. I put the letter to one side and stared hard at the I/C. So this was what a dead man looked like. There were shadows under his eyes. There was something far away in his expression, a face not prepared for the snap of the camera.

There was his name.

My name also. Separated from his by the word 'Bin'.

His race.

Date of birth.

Country of birth.

On the back, his I/C number.

Our home address.

But what absorbed me the most was a little hole that had been punched in his I/C. It was there to say that the I/C could no longer be used. To show someone an I/C like this, you would have to place your finger and thumb over the hole, praying that nobody would notice that you were holding something that had been damaged.

I suddenly saw my son holding the I/C this way, trying to pass himself off as someone who was still alive. It was just the sort of lying thing that I could expect from him. I imagined him doing it with that crooked smile on his face, the smile he always used to convince us that he would change, that he was listening, that everything would turn out all right. And I became angry.

My anger turned towards the person who had punched the hole. I had seen the way a credit card is destroyed, with a big pair of scissors slicing it into two halves. Why couldn't they do the same with this I/C? Why this clean, straightforward hole? I felt my anger burn, like a droplet of acid, first on my skin, through the flesh, right into my bones.

My son was no more. I saw a series of circles, perfect circles...the outline of a playground, the stone table under our block, the noose tightening around his neck, the shape of his mouth when he was still a baby, shrinking to the size of the hole. It was an opening through which I felt my body leaking, drop by drop, until the day I join my son on the other side.

The Bath

P ak° Zul was summoned to the house in the afternoon,
right after his Zohor° prayers. It was Malik, one of his
former students, who called him.

"We're not sure what to do, Pak Zul," Malik said.

"What's the problem?" Pak Zul asked.

"You'll have to come down and see."

When Pak Zul arrived, he noticed that there were very few
guests in the flat. He was introduced to the mother, a large
woman with shadows around her eyes, the colour of coffee
stains. She waddled towards him, swaying from side to side, as
if for her the act of walking was a painful uprooting of each foot
from the floor.

"Thank you for coming down, Pak Zul," she said. Pak Zul
was surprised by her voice, which was high, almost girlish. Was
that her natural voice or did hours of exhausted crying alter its
pitch? She then gestured to the kitchen, where Malik and his
assistants had gathered.

Pak Zul approached the metal tub in which the body was
laid. It was that of a man, probably in his thirties, though his
sunken cheeks made him look a lot older. Pak Zul recalled how
unnerved he used to be by the facial expressions of the dead—
because they were in actual fact the absence of expression.

He instructed Malik to remove the batik° sarong that was covering the body. Pak Zul's eyes widened as a curious sight greeted him: Malik had unveiled a leopard. All over the man's skin there were reddish, purplish spots. It seemed as if someone had stubbed cigarettes all over him, but from the inside, causing bumps to appear.

"We're not sure what precautions to take," Malik said. Pak Zul noticed that there were goosebumps on Malik's forearms. He checked his own forearms and realised they were there too.

He asked Malik, "You've all got your gloves, haven't you?"

"Yes," Malik replied. "But should we put on a double layer?"

"A single layer will do," said Pak Zul.

It was the first time that Pak Zul had encountered a corpse like this. He saw the word that was on the lips of everyone gathered around the tub. He saw the fear in their eyes, the fear that a disease could possibly survive a man's death.

Malik held the running hose as Pak Zul started to scrub the body, first from the right shoulder, down to the arm, the flank, the thigh, calf and foot. He repeated this for the left side. Initially, the texture of each lesion (even through the latex gloves) caused a shudder to shoot through Pak Zul's body, but by the time he had reached the man's left knee he could no longer feel any more spasms of disgust. He had broken into a sweat, and it mingled with a slight breeze to bring him calm.

Pak Zul then asked the assistants to raise the body at an angle. He massaged the man's stomach to vacate waste and gas. The man was so skinny that his waist was like the inner concave of a clamshell, roofed by the lower edges of his ribs. The assistants looked away as brownish fluid flowed between the slats the body was laid on, slapping onto the floor of the tub. This was drained by a hose leading into the bathroom.

A second round of washing involved soap, and a third one used water mixed with camphor. In time, Pak Zul's hands finally found the pressure he had often used to caress the dead. It was not too rough, as the body was still raw from the exit of the soul, but not too gentle either, because one still had to deal with less metaphysical matters, like dirt.

Finally the body was wrapped in white cloth, exposing only the face. Was there really no expression? Pak Zul knew that most of the time the expressions were what the living projected: serenity, or contentment. But since these bodies were strangers to him, the only expression he often saw was suffering. And there were those who had suffered more than others.

Pak Zul wondered which one caused the man greater suffering: the pain from his illness, or the fact that it was likely that people had shunned physical contact with him in the last years of his life. When Pak Zul walked into the living room, he had a word with the man's mother.

"We have bathed your son," he said. "He is now clean." What he meant to say was that strangers had touched the body, and so should the family. But Pak Zul had a feeling that they would know what to do. He hoped that at least someone would send the man off, as they often did, with a kiss on his forehead. He imagined this as the only mark on the man's body that the angels would see.

The Sendoff

Dahlan was one of two wardens they had identified to replace the ageing Mr Singh. When Dahlan first received the news, he sought out Mr Singh after the latter had finished one of his shifts. It was a Friday, and the two men sat in the prison canteen. From the windows, located high on the walls, one could see the dark blue sky. A stubborn crescent moon could be glimpsed, like a watermark left behind by a cup, soon to be erased by daylight.

"Mr Singh, I heard you nominated me. Who's the other guy?" Dahlan asked.

"I don't think you know him. He works in another prison."

"So why not choose him?"

"You're still my first choice, Dahlan. He's just a backup plan, in case you decide not to take on the job. But just between you and me, I don't really trust the fella. I heard he's got some debts, you know. Gambling debts or something. So, he might do it just because of the money."

Dahlan smiled. "And you think I won't?"

"I know you lah. If you do the job, you'll do it out of principle. We all have a part to play. When I was small, my mother will always say, if I don't study hard, I'll become a road sweeper. But can you imagine if nobody cleans the roads?"

"But what you're doing is much more serious than sweeping roads, Mr Singh."

"Of course. But because of what I do, Singapore is one of the safest places to live in. Whether it's to keep this country clean, or safe, someone has to do the dirty work."

Two days later, Dahlan was brought to a room, with a stove in one corner. There were two big metal pots on it. There was also a table, with bars of soap arranged in a row, their paper packaging still intact. Dahlan glanced at the design on the wrappers: a woman, in spaghetti straps, smiling radiantly.

"Here, my friend, is where you'll learn the ropes," Mr Singh chuckled. "People think it takes a real man to do what I do, but you can see that in here I'm just like a housewife. And this is my personal kitchen."

Mr Singh then explained to Dahlan that the rope had to be prepared by first boiling it, so that it would not become 'too springy'. And then the knot on the noose would be scrubbed with soap, to minimise friction. Dahlan asked why Mr Singh chose to use beauty soap.

"You want to make it easier for them. When you put the rope over their heads, I think it's nice to have this fragrance. It's comforting, don't you think?"

"But don't you put the cloth bag over their heads before you put on the noose? How can they smell anything through the bag?"

"Ah, that's the other thing that I do. I put a bar of soap inside those cloth bags. So it leaves a nice smell behind. You know, scientists have found out that nice smells can help you relax. Like aromatherapy."

Dahlan nodded absently. He tried to imagine what it was

like to have one's last breaths enveloped by a scent called—he glanced at the bars of soap again—'Petal Touch'.

"You don't have to do these things, actually. The main thing is to ensure that the rope is prepared properly. But I just like to put in a little bit extra for them."

Dahlan was then led to another room. Its centre was occupied by wooden flooring, with three trapdoors. Mr Singh showed him the metal ring hooks that were affixed on the floor and the ceiling.

"On the wall there you can see the three red buttons for the trapdoors. Very simple, labelled A, B, C."

Like some kind of game show, Dahlan thought to himself. With a laughing track, recorded by people who were now dead.

"Do you ever hang people three at a time?" he asked.

"Of course." Mr Singh replied. "It's more efficient. If we hang them one by one, we make everyone wait. Like the coroner. I don't think he likes to hang around this place for too long."

Dahlan ignored that attempt at levity. There was one live voice amidst that macabre laughing track, and it belonged to Mr Singh. "You mean there's struggling?"

"Sometimes. But most of the time it's instant. If you've done your calculations correctly, measured body weight and the rope length and all that, should be no problem. There was this one bugger who decided to go on hunger strike. We had to keep weighing him every week. Made my job difficult."

Later, at the canteen, Mr Singh began to elaborate on his profession, speaking between mouthfuls of rice and beef rendang.

"I don't believe in lethal injection, or firing range and all that. These are not natural methods, you know? The old-fashioned way is still the best. Because if you think about it, what's causing their death is their own body weight. You're not introducing anything foreign into their bodies. No poison, no bullets, no gas. And also, you give them a chance to do some good."

"What chance is that?"

"They can choose to donate their organs if they want."

"Mr Singh, how do you do it?"

Mr Singh sipped from his glass of tea. "I tell them something before I put on the noose. I say to them, 'I'm going to send you to a better place.' And for the ones who can reason, they see the truth in what I'm saying. It's better than staying in prison for the rest of your life."

"But how do you know it's going to be a better place? You're Muslim right? Then it's either heaven or hell. How do you know which one they're going to?"

"How do you know I'm a Muslim?"

"I heard you converted when you married a Malay woman. What does she think about your work?"

"She left me when she found out about what I did for a living."

Dahlan wanted to ask whether this meant that Mr Singh had also left the religion. But looking at Mr Singh's face, which had suddenly turned melancholic, he decided against it.

A week later, Dahlan handed in his resignation letter. He met with Mr Singh again, for what he hoped was the last time, at the canteen.

"I shouldn't have told you about my wife leaving me," Mr Singh said. Now you're afraid of how your family's going to treat you."

"Mr Singh, my wife passed away two years ago. I'm not in danger of anyone leaving me. If there's anything that I'm afraid of, it's of something else leaving me."

"What is it?"

"I don't know whether it's the right word, Mr Singh. But I think it is. It's my conscience."

"You didn't have to quit the service, you know. You've been with us for a long time. And you're going to miss out on your retirement benefits. So what are your plans now?"

Dahlan smiled. In a sense, he was thankful to Mr Singh for exposing the innards of the system, for showing him a darkness so potent that only those cursed with a kind of willful blindness could navigate through it.

"I'm sending myself to a better place."

Pasir Panjang, 3 PM

When she first walks into the Police Post, there is a vulnerability and tremulousness to her bearing that makes the officers on duty remark inwardly, "Whatever it is, she's innocent." They watch her as she looks at the Crime Prevention posters on the walls, her hands clutching her purse. It's dry outside but it seems as if she has walked in from the rain, such are the signals her body sends out, all the muffled appeals for warmth and contact. The officer whose rank is higher speaks first, "Can I help you?" The woman smiles enigmatically, shakes her head, and leaves, back into the sunlight.

That night, one of the officers (or perhaps both, for she was the kind of woman who makes men think the same thoughts) will file a Missed Person report before falling asleep.

A Howling

The first time Zaiton saw Sinta was when the latter was walking her employer's dog. Sinta was the domestic worker for the neighbours two houses down the street, a childless husband-and-wife couple in their 40's. Sinta herself was in her 20's, with a family consisting of a husband and two young children in Pacitan, East Java.

Zaiton and those neighbours were just nodding acquaintances, and all she knew of them was that the husband drove a big, maroon Mercedes-Benz, and that the wife did not cook. She deduced this from the fact that the car would leave the compound every evening, as the occupants of the house drove out for dinner.

She was watering the plants in her garden when Sinta approached her gate, smiling, while at the same time trying to restrain the dog. It was a German Shepherd, its tongue lolling out of the side of its mouth like a long, deflated pink balloon.

"Ibu, do you mind if I ask you something?"

To the Indonesians, 'Ibu' was an honorific for older women. In Malay, however, it was the term for 'mother'. Zaiton immediately felt a maternal affinity towards Sinta.

"What is it about?" Zaiton asked.

"I was wondering if you could tell me where I can find some clay around here."

"What do you need clay for?"

"I want to clean myself after handling the dog. I try not to touch it, but sometimes I can't avoid it."

Zaiton understood. Muslims were forbidden to come into contact with dogs, which were considered unclean animals. If one had touched a dog, then one had to perform a specific cleansing ritual, known as sertu. It involved washing the affected part not only with water several times, but also with a concoction of one part clay mixed with six parts of water.

"If it was back at my village I can find clay anywhere," Sinta said. "But around here I don't know where to look."

"I'll see what I can do," said Zaiton. "Why don't you come and see me this Sunday?"

On Sunday morning, Sinta visited Zaiton. Her employers had gone to church. Zaiton opened a plastic bag and took out three bars of soap, encased in individual white boxes.

"I went to Johor to get these," Zaiton said.

"What are they?"

"They're sertu soap," she replied, with a tinge of pride in her voice. "Things are very modern nowadays. The soap is mixed with the correct amount of clay and water. It's approved by the religious authorities in Malaysia."

"Thank you so much, Ibu," Sinta said. "I had just given the dog a bath this morning."

Zaiton tried to control herself from showing displeasure on her face. She asked Sinta, "Do you mean that your employers make you wash the dog?"

"The dog can't wash itself."

"I know that," said Zaiton. "But don't they know that you're a Muslim? Do you pray at home?"

"Of course," Sinta replied. And to prove that she did, she pointed towards Zaiton's kitchen and said, "That's the direction towards Mecca, right?"

"Correct. If you need any prayer mats or whatever you can tell me. We have a lot in this house."

The week after, Zaiton met with Sinta again. She told Sinta that as a fellow Muslim, she was concerned that Sinta had to manage the dog as part of her duties.

"I've spoken to my husband," Zaiton said. "Even though we don't really need a maid, we don't mind being your employers if you want to leave that house."

"But Ibu," Sinta said. "I've been using your soap. There's really no problem."

"Yes, Sinta," Zaiton said. "But using the soap isn't going to get rid of the real problem. The problem is that your employers care more for their dog than they care about you."

The next evening, Sinta's employer turned up at Zaiton's gate. When she recognised him, Zaiton started to panic. She did not like confrontations. Now the man would start telling her to mind her own business.

"I'm sorry, my husband is not in," was the first thing she said to him.

"I'd like to have a talk with you, actually," said the man. He was wearing a shirt and long pants, as if he had just arrived home from work. Zaiton invited him into the house and served him some tea.

"I know we haven't really introduced ourselves," the man

said. "My name is Wee Keong. My wife's name is Lindy. She wanted to come today, but she's at her counselling session."

"My name is Zaiton. Your wife is a counsellor?"

"No, she's not. I think I'll get straight to the point. Today Sinta told me that she wants to work for you. And she said it had something to do with the dog."

"Muslims are not supposed to touch dogs," said Zaiton.

"I know that," said Wee Keong. "And we did ask her from the beginning whether she was comfortable with it."

"If she said she's not comfortable then you won't give her the job."

"Madam Zaiton, we really like Sinta, even if she's just been with us for a month. If she doesn't want to take care of the dog, it's fine with us. But she's a great cook."

Somehow, Zaiton felt relieved. She was having second thoughts about the cost of hiring Sinta.

"My wife stopped cooking after our son died. It reminded her too much of him. She wanted to get rid of all the things that brought back memories of him. The only thing we couldn't get rid of was the dog. Because the dog was the boy's favourite thing in the world. And I know it's stupid to say this but I sometimes think there's a bit of our son that lives in him. Because unlike our son's books, or his toys, this thing... he's alive, you know?"

"It's not stupid," Zaiton said.

"So what I wanted to say is...the dog, to us, is more than just an animal. Sometimes when he howls at night I feel that he understands my wife and myself more than any other person can. But at the same time we've never treated Sinta as anything less than one of us."

"I'm sorry," Zaiton said. "I didn't know."

Wee Keong rose to leave. The confession had left him somewhat drained. "Sorry for taking up your time. If your family is free I'd like to ask you round for dinner. Sinta only cooks halal food."

"Anyway, what's his name?"

"Our son? Andrew."

It wasn't the answer that Zaiton expected. She had wanted to ask for the dog's name, as if that would lead her to understand Wee Keong's loss. She decided to ask Sinta the next time. Then she would try to figure out—the boy's name, the name of the dog—which one was the echo of which.

A *Pontianak Story*

In the month of September in 2001, he met a woman who was a resident at the Institute of Mental Health, where he was posted for his psychiatry attachment. She was an attractive lady, in her 30's, her long hair tied in a ponytail. When she sat opposite him in the interview room, she placed her hands in a stately manner on the edge of the table, much like how a Malay bride would display her henna-stained fingers on an embroidered cushion.

"They cut my fingernails," she informed him, as if an explanation was required for her stiff pose. Her brittle dignity suggested to him a naked woman explaining how her clothes had been taken away.

She answered his questions politely: her date of birth, marital status, her place of origin. She could accurately tell him the day's date, month, and year, as well as her present surroundings. And then, as if to prevent him from being lulled into routine data collection, she voluntarily offered to him the date and circumstances of her death.

It was three years ago, she claimed, when she had blacked out after giving birth to her child. An uncontrollable episode of postpartum haemorrhage was the coroner's report. As for her child, it (she was unsure of its sex) too failed to survive, on account of its premature status. As her family was not wealthy, mother and child were buried in the same plot. Furthermore, since they were not superstitious, they had failed to observe the proper precautionary rites, which included placing an egg in her mouth and two under her armpits.

True enough, when she woke up, she found ample space in her mouth for the growth of fangs. These, she claimed, could be retracted at will, like a cat's claws. Also, with her arms unimpeded by eggs, she had managed to wrestle free from her confines of tight-swaddled white and batik cloth, as well as her canopy of packed earth. She found that that same lightness which had allowed her to seep between particles of loam also allowed her to climb the air—gravity for her was no longer a law, but a toy.

And like a perverse version of the Prophet's ascendancy to the seventh heavens from Jerusalem on the night of the Mi'raj˙, she had her own visions as she travelled vertically through the soil: of beetles whose multi-segmented bodies and innumerable legs made them undulate as smoothly as black lacquered tongues, of hermaphroditic worms which seemed to telescope in two opposite directions, torn as they were from the pulls of conflicting libidos, of the lattice of roots forming its own network of roads and aqueducts in a subterranean city.

Her first task, it seemed, was to seek nourishment for her child, who as it turned out, had been returned to her womb. But she would take no chances this time—during her first pregnancy, the problem was a kind of placental insufficiency, which denied her foetus adequate nourishment. It was her maternal duty to now seek redress for this; she would hunt for sources of transfusion.

The student scribbled furiously, devouring every detail. He knew that much of what she said was technically redundant, since he had already landed on a provisional diagnosis: delusion, with possible schizophrenia (he would need to find out later if she was also prone to auditory hallucinations). But in the margins he had written his own notes:

'Fascinating. Patient actually believes she is a pontianak. Re: Malay ghost who died during childbirth. Interesting how she perceives ghost's blood thirst as retaliatory. Against what? Her inseminator—a man, and hence all men? Or against fate, which claimed two lives during an act initially designed to bring life into the world? Must write about this. An encounter in an asylum where instead of a Self becoming the Other (diagnosed, filed, exiled from the 'normal'), here I meet someone who has made the Other (a figure of superstition) a figure sitting just opposite my table: humanised, with a subjectivity, a countenance, and a voice! Can also write about feminism: bloodsucking as draining the phallus of its hydraulic fuel. Hence male panic and impotence.'

After his interview (she did indeed experience auditory hallucinations, although these were in the form of the famished wails of a baby), the student thanked the patient and proceeded to the trolley where the case files were kept. He had already fulfilled his daily quota of case interviews, but he was curious as to what other characters roamed this serendipitous ward he had been assigned to. In his lab coat, and with a stethoscope slung around his neck, he looked like any other medical student. The nocturnal secret he kept from the patients was that he was also a writer, who wanted to hear their stories because he too wanted to feed his own child—a voracious imagination. He would be the first to admit that it was an act which could only be described, in its neediness and duplicity, as vampiric.

The Barbershop

We made a makeshift barbershop in front of our bunk, along the corridor.

I was seated bare-bodied on a folding chair, directly under a fluorescent lamp. No mirrors placed in front and behind me to replicate my image towards diminishing eternity. No rectangle of cloth pegged at the back of my neck. No TV screen playing football matches. No stereo system blaring dangdut° songs, with those distinctive bass beats that sound like the frenzied burst of magma bubbles. No electric shearers caressing my head, its serrated nib so close to my scalp I could feel my skull vibrating drowsily. And none of those after-cut treats: the chill of rosewater lathered along my mandible by a shaving brush, the razor blade scratching against my sideburn follicles in that most satisfying manner: along the grain.

"Boss, how you want?" Sudin asked. Sudin was a storeman from the QM branch. I was a sergeant from Bravo company. We had both been confined for the weekend; him, for losing one of the brushes from his rifle-cleaning kit, and myself, for forgetting to sign the book in/book out book.

I noticed something as Sudin snipped my hair and itchy tufts fell on my bare shoulders. I had an urge to talk. My memories of haircuts, when I was a child, and teenager, was one of humiliation. I visited a Malay barbershop near my old home in Tampines, one called Bugs Bunny but which had, in addition to the eponymous rabbit, pictures of Woody Woodpecker on the glass doors. One might think that the environment would have been one that was child-friendly. After sitting down on a cushioned plank placed across armrests, I would then be asked in which style I wanted my hair to be cut.

This was when terror would strike me, unfailingly. Because the question would be delivered in Malay, and I couldn't answer in Malay. I was scoring quite distinguished Mother Tongue grades in school, but when it came to banter, I found myself rummaging through a mental dictionary. Furthermore, it was a dictionary submerged in water, soaked to the spine, its pages wrinkled and warped. The very act of diving to retrieve such a wreck involved breathlessness and the deceleration experienced when one enters another medium. What words to choose without sounding stilted or straying to silence in mid-sentence?

In retrospect though, I think it was my fear of not getting the inflections right that paralysed me, more so than a lexical poverty. Maybe I knew the words to use, how to string them together, but had no idea how to achieve that unreachable diction that would disguise the fact that these very words had been frantically translated from English.

So I would answer in English: cut the sides short, don't cut so much at the top, leave a slope at the back. There was one time, though, when the barber frowned and asked sarcastically, "You don't know how to speak Malay, is it?" I remember blushing when those words pierced me, my ears turning red, wishing the barber wasn't so close as to notice such obvious signs of shame. That was the longest haircut of my life; staring into the mirror I saw a boy who, quite simply, didn't belong.

There were other customers sitting on the bench outside: there were old men in white songkok Haji°, boys in soccer T-shirts, Mat Motors° in their sunglasses and windbreakers, one with his helmet decorated with a sticker of a pair of Mercurial wings. When these people came in, they would smile at the barbers, call them abang (brother) or nak (child) with familiarity and ease. There would be nothing alien about the barbers' mullets, nicotine-stained teeth, pious goatees or the stone-encrusted rings on their fingers. I wasn't part of this network of easy rapport—my feet didn't touch the hair-carpeted floor, my disembodied head was hovering in the air, cut off at the neck by a white sheet. A ghost, rootless, not of these customs and hence not of this world.

Haircuts became rituals of retreat. The snips of scissors and hum of electric shearers carried out dialogues around my head, and all the while I was submerging myself in a private silence, a stone dropped in a dark well, shrinking like my own reflection endlessly multiplied by the front and back mirrors. The closer the blades got to my scalp, the further I withdrew into my mind's sanctum.

But hair grows. And what was severed is replaced, finds its own length.

So back again to last night, where I had Sudin hovering around me, snipping away. Another barbershop, another chance at redemption. As all the dead weight fell around me, accumulating in a black halo at my feet, I spoke about falling in love again, about the directions one takes in one's life, how sometimes detours can take you full circle.

I spoke first in Malay, and then unconsciously switched

to English. It didn't matter. I was being understood. And I thought of that barber from Bugs Bunny, who oppressed a twelve-year-old and initiated a cycle of self-recrimination, with his disgust at my inadequate grasp of the language. Living in Singapore for so long, and having served customers of many races, was it even possible that he could not have comprehended my English? I thought of all the purists who appoint themselves as the linguistic police, who insist on rigid notions of cultural authenticity.

A humble pair of paper scissors. My hesitant Malay, my over-mannered English. As I admired my hair in the mirror later on, I thought: never judge the handiwork from the tools.

Bukit Batok, 5 PM

With their slippers as goalposts, four boys play soccer with a plastic ball; a ball with what looks like a scar across its side, and a navel where the air which gave it its shape might have entered; which skitters rather than bounces. Their field is a void deck, whose floor coats their soles with ovals of grey. When one of them scores a goal, an imaginary stadium roars euphorically, a multitude of streamers and flags flashing like the jingles of a tambourine.

They play until dusk, when it is time to return to their homes. A chorus of voices receives them: "How many times do I have to tell you, once you step into the house go straight to the toilet!" "Play until don't know when to come back, is it?" "What were you doing until you got your knees so black?" "When you come back at this time you invite the devil in!" HDB life: one takes the stairs and elevators up to be brought back down to earth.

His Birthday Present

Nur Jannah always told her son, Shafiq, to make friends with the Chinese boys. She said, "If you have Malay friends, you'll always be talking. You won't know what the teacher is saying." She believed that Shafiq would pick up some of the habits of the Chinese by mixing around with them. For her, this meant a competitive spirit and a natural aptitude in Maths.

Since her divorce, Nur Jannah had been making dresses to supplement her income as a food stall assistant in the day. In the evening, when Shafiq looked up from his books, he would see his mother hunched over her electric sewing machine, the light from its pilot lamp glinting off her spectacles.

One day, Shafiq came home from school with a plastic bag of some chocolate bars and candy. Before Nur Jannah could start scolding him, he explained that a boy was giving them out because of his upcoming birthday party. She asked him what race he was, and whether Shafiq had been invited.

The next day, Shafiq came to class and asked the boy, Terence, whether he could go to his birthday party. Shafiq was shy, but did as his mother had drilled him: he told Terence that he had bought a birthday gift and could he please go to Terence's house to present it to him. Terence gave Shafiq his home address, and throughout the day kept on pestering Shafiq to tell him what the gift was. Shafiq replied that it was a 'secret', but the truth was that he had no idea.

During the party, Nur Jannah realised that she and Shafiq were the only Malay family present. It was her first time visiting a bungalow and she found a corner for herself in the balcony, under some hanging pots of ferns. One of the women sat beside Nur Jannah and started a conversation. She introduced herself as Terence's aunt.

"My English not so good," Nur Jannah said.

The woman looked puzzled. As if sensing that his mother was in some kind of danger, Shafiq appeared, holding a plate of fried vermicelli.

"Shafiq, you can't eat this," Nur Jannah said.

The woman chuckled. "Don't worry, there's no pork. The hot dog is chicken."

"No," Nur Jannah replied. "He eat this later he get stomachache. Shafiq, you wait for the cake later OK?"

After the cake was cut, Terence entertained everyone with a short recital on a baby grand piano in the living room. He then opened his presents, and squealed excitedly when he unveiled a PlayStation set. Among his other presents were a railway set, a Lego fire station, and a remote-controlled racing car. Nur Jannah grabbed Shafiq to leave before Terence could finish unwrapping all his presents. She thanked the hosts and told them that Shafiq was not feeling well.

Later that night, after brushing his teeth, Shafiq asked Nur Jannah, "Mama, can I have a piano?"

Nur Jannah looked up from her sewing. "Why?"

"So I can play in a concert and make a lot of money. And then I can give you the money and you don't have to work anymore."

"We don't have money for a piano."

Shafiq bit his lip. "Then can I have a gun?"

"What gun, sayang°?"

"The big water gun that you bought for Terence. But I want the blue one. Blue is my favourite colour."

"No, Shafiq."

"Why?"

She wanted to tell him that her way of showing love for her child was not through buying toys. It had to do with the pity in her breast when she watched him leave for school each morning, walking down the lonely corridor, shifting his shoulders from side to side so that the weight of his box-like backpack could be centralised. She remembered one day when he turned around, unexpectedly, to smile at her, and how she had to force her hand to clench a goodbye wave. It was a hand that was going to cover her mouth, to stifle a sob; she had felt at that moment that she did not deserve to have Shafiq in her life.

But all she could say was, "Because you're my son."

Foreign Language

Maisarah met Jacques at a night class for Arabic. Recently, in the course of her work at the archives, she had been tasked to translate the contents of 1950s Malay entertainment magazines. Maisarah had discovered that her Jawi, acquired in her teens during Sunday religious classes, was rusty. She then decided to study the alphabet again, with the acquisition of a new vocabulary as an added bonus.

Jacques, on the other hand, had enrolled to 'deepen' his 'understanding of Islam'. He had converted a year ago, after the death of his wife. It was a colleague at the International School where he taught who had passed him an anthology of Sufi writing, and he had found in them both solace and inspiration. When Jacques told her this, Maisarah had felt uncomfortable, for she was not wearing a tudung.

Maisarah was forty and single. Among her relatives, her uncovered hair was rationalised by the fact that she had yet to settle into married life. But she did not like what it also insinuated: that she was waiting to be rescued by a man who would wind her up, like an obedient toy, and set her down the path of piety. The tudung then seemed to be something she withheld, almost sulkily, to spite her fate.

She told Jacques how, to the Malays, fate had many children. There was rezeki, which meant one's fortune (including offspring). There was ajal, the hour of one's death. And then there was jodoh, which was one's intended in life. It was a word designed to shift the concept of singlehood away from what made it so nervous and so brittle: that one was overlooked, bypassed, rejected. Her match had simply not made an appearance in her life.

When her two younger sisters were about to get married, they had teased her about having to offer her compensation— for the fact that they had 'crossed the threshold', or langkah bendul.

"They have to buy you a present, because you're not supposed to get married before your older siblings," Maisarah explained. "But I told them I didn't want anything. It's embarrassing."

"I would have just grabbed the money and run. There's nothing to be embarrassed about."

She wondered if Jacques was then starting to view her as some kind of exotic curiosity. Maybe he was thinking of the culture she came from, with its overwrought notions of honour and shame. He was contrasting it with his own, encapsulated in the blasé idiom he had just employed. But Maisarah herself was noticing the casual, unguarded way he looked over her shoulder at her worksheet, his faded blue eyes and ash-blond hair, and his French-Canadian accent, which she often tried to imitate on her walk to the bus stop after class.

Maisarah had never been able to tell her parents that all their well-meaning attempts at matchmaking were futile, because she felt no attraction towards Malay men. She had been on dates before, with Malay professionals, ranging from an airline pilot to a dentist, and despite her emphatic nods and fond smiles, felt lost and vacant. Often, she would shake her head after laughing, and behind this disguise of being satiated by a joke was a secret soliloquy that said, "I'm so sorry, but you're not the one. You're not the one at all."

Could this estrangement have been a product of her education at an all-girls missionary school? For two years she was in love with a Eurasian boy (with a New Zealander mother) from an affiliated school. He was the vice-captain of his school rugby team. Her contact with him, however, was completely vicarious; the boy was dating her best friend. As a confidant, Maisarah was treated to thrilling examples of his serious, fumbling courtship. In private, Maisarah simply substituted herself in her best friend's place, except that she slipped into a more hopeless detour. The boy was Catholic, and Maisarah wallowed, or luxuriated, in the impossibility of their union, unsure afterwards how to distinguish the two. "Love," she had once written, "is what happens to other people," and she read it like an ecstatic, liberating insight.

It was this fidelity to this Eurasian boy, she reasoned, that had made her so easily disappointed with her parents' choices. She had once registered an online profile on a site for 'East-West' connections, But she found herself feeling alienated by other women who found Caucasian men more 'romantic, witty, charming', because what she was seeking was not someone she deemed culturally superior, but someone who was culturally unfeasible. After a week she deactivated her account.

So she did know what to make of Jacques: polite, ironic, a year older than her, and who had lately been suggesting a dinner date. Because he was of the same religion, it compromised the remoteness she thought essential to her developing feelings for him. Sometimes she fantasised about joining another language class in the future—a French class.

At which level would she be able to write a competent love letter? She would write to his home address in Brossard, Quebec, to surprise and impress him. But what she relished most was the idea that such a letter would not be sent, never be sent. Nobody would see it, not even to disinterestedly correct its naïve grammar.

One night, during after-class supper, Maisarah told Jacques that she did not see herself as a certain stereotype: that of the woman who preferred men who were not of her own race. She could not help but feel a certain shame attached to it, as if she had dishonoured her own brothers. Eventually, she also told Jacques about the Eurasian boy, and the insurmountable barrier that would stand between them if they were to ever pursue a romantic route.

"I think you're just trying to protect yourself," Jacques finally said. "You want to be able to place certain causes— if you're looking for causes—on what race you are, your religion. Just in case the other person doesn't love you back. You want to be able to pinpoint why you're the wrong type for someone, even though the idea of type is often a mystery."

Maisarah felt invaded, but also illuminated, by what Jacques had said.

"They won't get in the way if you don't let them. You can brush them aside. It's not so hard for me to understand what jodoh is, for example. There's nothing alien about it. Love that is destined. Le destin nous a réunis."

"What should I do?" she asked.

"Just be Maisarah."

All this time she had asked Jacques to call her Sarah, and now he was calling her 'my Sarah'. It struck her a few seconds later that he was merely telling her to be herself. She blushed furiously.

Jacques noticed the colour rise to her cheeks. Hastily and mercifully, he said, "Oh, that too."

Maisarah concentrated on the less risky meaning: the advice to just be who she was. But she knew that what she really wanted, glancing at Jacques' open, smiling face, was to be the 'other people' a younger Maisarah once wrote about.

Reunion

Saleha started on a diet, recommended by her sister, two weeks before her school reunion dinner. It involved the consumption of powdered Indonesian herbs, called jamu. Saleha's husband, Majid, asked her, "Does it work?"

"It only works for women," Saleha snapped. "You don't try it ah? I'm going to hide it."

"I'm not asking to try it," Majid replied. "I'm just asking if you can see the effects after two weeks."

"Don't think I don't know that you've been taking my primrose oil tablets. You can't resist seeing pills lying around."

"What, you don't like to see your husband healthy like you?"

Saleha stirred the jamu in a glass. It had a lurid colour, like moss. She dreaded having to swallow it.

"Majid Bin Mokhtar, that primrose oil is for women with menopause. They're not vitamins!"

Saleha knew that their school reunions made Majid insecure. In her time, Saleha had been one of the popular beauties at school, a status she attained despite not being a member of any of the prominent extra-curricular groups. In fact, she was blissfully unaware of how she was perceived by her schoolmates, until the news arrived that the Raja

Permaisuri Agong, wife of the Sultan of Malaysia, would visit the school.

Her form teacher then approached her to ask if she would like to present a bouquet to the Queen herself on the occasion. Singapore had joined the Federation of Malaysia just two months ago, and their school, being the first Malay-medium secondary school established on the island, held special significance for the royal visit. Saleha later found out that there was an unofficial nomination form that circulated around school, and that her name was the most cited.

Two weeks later, when they entered the car, Saleha noticed that Majid was wearing some scent. She had never known him to buy any fragrance for himself, apart from the sandalwood-based atar that he dabbed on his garments for Friday prayers.

"Do you remember the Queen's visit?" Saleha suddenly asked.

"Yah," Majid replied. "Why?"

"What was her name?"

"I don't recall. It started with 'B'. Was it 'Bedah'?"

Saleha slapped her husband's shoulder.

"Don't!" Majid said. "I'm driving!"

"What kind of name is that? Bedah is the name of some kampung woman who makes keropok*!"

"But it really starts with 'B'. Anyway, what does it matter?"

Saleha had raised the matter precisely because she wanted Majid to remember her as she was on that day: fifteen, in a white school uniform starched for the occasion, blue ribbons in her plaits. She had a whole line of suitors then, from Kamal, who was now a newspaper editor, to Abdul

Ghani, who later became a secondary school headmaster. But she had given her hand to Majid, who was the top student in her class. Whoever could have predicted that he would end up working as an electrician with the Public Utilities Board, and later a taxi driver, while she herself took on jobs in factories to supplement their income?

The reunion was held at a ballroom of a small hotel. The Master of Ceremonies began with a pantun*, about separation and longing. He elaborated on it by stating that each reunion was an opportunity to keep the spirit of the school alive, since its closure in the late 1980s. The food menu was like that at a wedding, with briyani rice, pickled vegetables and curry. To Saleha's satisfaction, she was asked to pose for photographs more times than Majid. She congratulated herself for sticking to her diet, which made her lose two kilograms in two weeks. Majid seemed content to stay in his seat with a fixed, indulgent smile on his face.

On the way home, Majid remarked, "I saw you talking a lot to Kamal just now."

"He's so good to his wife. They went for holiday a few months ago. To Bali."

"If only you had married him," Majid said. "He could have given you a better life."

It was like that after every school reunion dinner, every year. All Saleha wanted was to rouse from Majid a spark of jealousy, which she believed, at her age, was the closest she could get to feeling desired. And yet sometimes she wondered if she had gone too far, and whether she had genuinely hurt Majid in the process.

For Majid, however, these conversations were just the shards of shattered aspirations; prickly, but essentially harmless. Their school was built in 1961, the year the government announced that the Malay School Certificate would be accepted as equivalent to the Cambridge School Certificate. The Education Minister had hailed it as 'a clear sign that colonial education is dead in Singapore'. Prior to this, there were Malay-language lessons broadcast on radio, Malay instated as the national language, free primary school education for Malays. The office of the Head of State, called the Yang di-Pertuan Negara, had been passed from a British governor to a Malay journalist.

Nobody could have blamed Majid then for envisioning a bright future for himself, especially since he was the top Science student in school. The fierce confidence with which he pursued Saleha then, the towering promises that he made to her...

And then Separation happened. English was promoted nationwide. As it turned out, the ones who had studied Arts ended up the more successful— here was still a demand for language teachers and vernacular journalists. But Majid's certificate lost its value overnight, and joined the ranks of the 'banana money' issued during the Japanese Occupation. Better these annual reunions, Majid thought, strained as they were, than the bitter dream of a reunion that would never take place. Better for Saleha to imagine her life in another house than a life in another country.

"Budriah," Majid suddenly said.

"What?"

"I remember now. Her name was Tengku° Budriah. The Queen. She was from the Royal House of Perlis."

"Perlis," Saleha repeated thoughtfully. "We've never been there before. I wonder what's there?"

"Maybe we can visit the palace," Majid said.

"She must be very old by now. Maybe she's passed away."

"Who cares about the Queen? I didn't even notice her. I only paid attention to the princess who gave her flowers."

Saleha looked away. Majid knew that a smile was spreading irresistibly across her lips. An idea occurred to him: tomorrow, after buying breakfast, he would visit the florist on the way home.

Bedok, 7 PM

A nother loaded bus zooms past the bus stop, as the three women glance at their wristwatches, almost simultaneously. They are wearing their blue factory uniforms, which is an exact shade of the transitory twilight sky at that very moment, although this observation is lost to them.

The woman who is leaning against the railing has a mother who has had a stroke and is now confined to a wheelchair. The woman who stands near the road is thinking of what to cook for her daughter who had just returned home the day before after disappearing for three weeks. The woman on the bus stop seat has just been proposed to by a Malaysian Chinese co-worker who has promised to convert to Islam, although she wonders whether his conversion to another nationality will be as plausible, considering his income.

Another bus approaches, and the three women turn to look at it, as if at their respective futures, hoping this one will have space for them.

A Toyol Story

It began one day when Fadly's father stood at the doorway to his bedroom to ask if he had seen his pair of spectacles. Fadly glanced at his father, replied that he had not, and went back to reading his comics. A moment later, he suddenly recalled that he had seen his father wearing them, and walked out into the living room. His father had overturned cushions, created a haphazard footpath from magazines, and was sweeping an oar-like hand across the limbo of dust balls, oxidised coins and beetle husks under the sofa. Red-faced from exertion, he looked up at Fadly and declared, "I think there's a toyol in our house." His spectacles, in mock gold, were sitting mockingly on his nose.

Malay superstition has it that a toyol is a kind of changeling, a stillborn foetus brought back to life by black magic, and condemned to do the bidding of its master in return for its unfortunate resurrection. Its primary occupation is mischief: petty theft, random rearrangement of private property, relentless harassment of routine. The most effective way to use a toyol on your enemy is through psychological warfare, the desired target being the victim's sense of reality. Let the victim's mind be under pressure from the combined burden of minute mysteries, a kind of Japanese water torture where a single drop of water, directed repeatedly at a precise point on the forehead, produced the most excruciating migraine. Drip: the unsolved case of the missing thimble. Drip: the drawer that gobbled up pen caps. Drip: the self-unlocking front door.

In the next few weeks, Fadly's father would complain of various vanishings: a particular segment of the newspaper, his favourite comb, as well as a pair of bathroom slippers. Hiding a growing sense of dread under a frosty icing of impatience, Fadly would explain how the Classifieds section had been used as a makeshift plate for the cat's dinner, that the comb had been left in the bathroom when his father was dyeing his hair black, and that the slippers had been thrown away a week ago, since the soles had been exhausted to the smoothness of fish-bellies. His tense replies, however, could not shake his father's belief that there was indeed some sorcery at work, in the form of an invisible, elfish intruder, whose operations were stealthier than electricity.

Inwardly, Fadly felt that his name was going to be called up soon from the register of filial sons. It was a summons as inescapable as being called up for National Service or vaccination. Fadly considered himself to be a reasonably respectful child, yet at the same time he feared the kinds of emotionally-draining adjustments he had to make in the light of his father's inverse puberty. He waited, in agitation, for the definitive sign that his father's increasing absentmindedness had spilled over into irrevocable senility. He knew that if that day were to arrive, his response would be a mixture of horror, fatalism and terrible loneliness—that between the two of them, only Fadly would be able to recognise the father's mental decline.

In the meantime, he started entertaining his father's theories that there was, indeed, a toyol in the house. "Yes," he replied to his father's laments, "someone out there is doing this to us." Fadly somehow believed that having faith in his father's system of delusions could delay his confrontation with the inevitable. "Yes," he would say sadly, watching the old man swear for the umpteenth time the last location of the remote control, "this house is being disturbed."

Fadly's father, encouraged by his son's reluctant support, started laying snares for the toyol. He bought a set of mousetraps, which he placed around the house; anywhere he figured where the hands of a kleptomaniac imp might wander. And thus it happened one day, while reading comics (although this time with an almost desperate absorption), that Fadly heard a cry from the kitchen. He rushed out of his bedroom to find his father sitting cross-legged on the floor and prying open a mousetrap that had clamped over his left big toe. Fadly's father was sobbing, a look of bewildered hurt on his face. In a voice peevish and shrunken, he asked Fadly, "Who put this damned thing here?"

Fadly knelt beside his father, put a hand on his shoulder, and said firmly, "Your toyol did, Pak." He had meant it as his habitual lie, but Fadly could have not been more struck by the truth in his words.

Second Take

There was a problem when the camera crew arrived at Pak Jumat's one-room flat. The director told him that his house was 'too clean'. They asked him if he could revert the house to its original state.

"That time you said that there's not going to be room for the camera and lights," Pak Jumat said.

"Don't worry," the director replied. "That's for us to handle. So, maybe we come back in the next few days?"

Pak Jumat sighed. He had spent the weekend actually shifting his stuff to his neighbour's house—the stand fan whose drooping neck was bandaged with black gaffer tape, piles of newspapers, old biscuit tin cans, a trolley, and a rack filled with wire baskets that held all the trinkets that Pak Jumat had not managed to sell at the Sungei Road flea market. Now he had to shift it all back.

He had knocked on Keong's door the week before, to ask if he could use the latter's house for temporary storage. They had not spoken to each other since an argument a few years ago, when Pak Jumat was accused of cluttering up the corridor. Surprisingly, Keong had agreed.

Keong was blind, and his house was sparsely furnished. Pak Jumat was very careful not to rearrange Keong's things as he stacked his own items in one corner of the living room area. The curtains to Keong's sleeping area (one could not call it a bedroom, since there was no wall partition) had been drawn aside, and Pak Jumat had noticed a small television placed beside a foam mattress.

During the shoot, Pak Jumat was instructed to sit on his bed, and some of the crew adjusted the position of objects in the background. A make-up artist dabbed some sweat off Pak Jumat's brow. The sound operator slipped a hand under Pak Jumat's shirt and clipped a tiny microphone near his collar. They did all this briskly, but he imagined that there was some tenderness in their gestures.

Pak Jumat almost broke into a smile when the lights were turned on and the camera started rolling. He would be on television for the first time in his life. But he managed to maintain a serious expression on his face.

A few weeks later, Pak Jumat visited Keong's house to watch himself on TV. To his disappointment, the picture on Keong's screen was shaking terribly. All he could see were images sliced into ribbons, with glimpses of faces, but coloured purple or green. Pak Jumat tried adjusting the aerial, but it was no use.

"Keong," Pak Jumat said, "You know or not your TV spoil?"

"How I know? I just listen to the sound only."

Pak Jumat was ready to leave. The show was in Mandarin, and there was little point in him staying on. But Keong started to translate for him.

"The hosts are talking right now," said Keong. "They're welcoming the guests-of-honour. And they're telling the viewers the number to call if they want to donate."

It was half an hour into the show, and Pak Jumat's segment had yet to appear. In the meantime, Keong had described which TV stars were appearing, and how much money had been raised. Pak Jumat noticed that Keong looked especially animated. This was probably the first time that Keong was helping someone else to see.

"I think you're on now," said Keong. "You're saying that you live alone. Your wife died and you don't have children. And you have sweet urine sickness."

"What's that?" It came to him within a second. "Oh, diabetes ah?"

Pak Jumat asked Keong if he wanted to have some Marie biscuits. The TV crew had given him a food hamper for agreeing to the interview.

"You mean they never give you money ah?" Keong replied. "You help them one, you know? People hear your story and then got more calls coming in."

Pak Jumat's mind wandered to the time when he was a child, dunking Marie biscuits in Milo. Depending on the cup's diameter, a side of his biscuit would be darkened, and it would look like one of the phases of the moon. Keong and Pak Jumat were old men now, so they dipped their biscuits in rich, black coffee. Pak Jumat's doctor had warned him against indulging in coffee, but he believed this was a special occasion.

"You also don't have many friends," he heard Keong's voice say. "Your friends all live far away."

Pak Jumat decided that he would take the whole hamper to Keong's house. He had yet to unwrap it, but had glimpsed through the orange cellophane wrapping a fruitcake, tinned peaches, butter cookies. He would let Keong choose what to open and eat. He didn't want to let Keong wait too long for him. Keong deserved better company than an accidental radio.

The Drawer

I lied to Maria this morning. I told her that I had not seen her tudung. I was supposed to iron the ensemble she was going to wear for her interview: her baju kurung dress and long skirt, and a matching cream tudung.

As Maria was putting on her clothes, I heard her cry out, "Mak, where's my tudung?"

"Tudung?" I asked. "Which one?"

"I'm already late, Mak. Where is it?"

"Why do you want to wear your tudung? Your hair isn't fully dried yet."

Maria walked out of the ironing room and glared at me. "So what if it's not dry?" she said. "It's my hair." She went into her bedroom and I followed her. She opened her drawers and threw out various scarves. It looked like a magic show that had gone very wrong.

"Why are you messing up the room like this?"

"I'll clean it when I get back. I'm late, Mak!"

I stood at the doorway, wondering how to phrase what I had been meaning to tell her for the past few months. Maria had already picked out a light yellow tudung.

"Maria, you've gone for so many interviews already. All your friends who graduated with you have already found jobs. I feel so sorry for you, but I don't know how to help you.

Just for today, why don't you try not wearing your tudung? You can wear it again after they've given you the job."

"I can't just put it on and take it off like that."

Maria left in a huff after taking some cab money from me, and left me to lock the gate. I watched her from the window as a taxi stopped for her. Somehow I imagined that as she slammed the door shut, a corner of her tudung got caught in the door. I have never seen such a thing happen before, but I pictured her anger like this small flag being whipped in the wind.

A few hours later I was at my sister's house, helping her to pluck bean sprouts. A translucent nest of roots was being formed on a piece of newspaper. My sister apparently noticed that I was plucking the roots too close to the stems.

"Don't waste," she said. "We can eat that part, you know."

"My mind's on other things," I said. "I'm waiting for Maria to call."

"Has she found a job yet?"

"She hasn't," I said. "All these job advertisements keep asking for people who speak Mandarin."

"What to do," my sister sighed. "It's become their country."

When my sister sent me off at the door, she asked if Maria would consider giving tuition classes to her son. She must have forgotten what I knew: that she sends her son to Mendaki° tuition on weekends. I thanked her as she passed me some mee soto° for dinner later.

On the cab ride home, I started thinking about my sister lying to me about her son's tuition. I had also done the same thing with Maria earlier, when I hid her tudung in a drawer in my room. But God would know that our intentions were good. Maybe Maria finally listened to me and at the last minute decided not to wear her tudung for her interview. My sister was right; this had become their country and one had to play by their rules.

My handphone suddenly rang. When I answered it, I heard Maria's voice excitedly telling me...the music in the cab was loud, so I told the driver to turn it down. Maria informed me, almost breathlessly, that she had been offered a job. I reminded her to say thanks to God and secretly in my heart felt that my own prayers had been answered.

After Maria hung up, the taxi driver restored the volume of the radio. A Chinese song started issuing from the speakers just behind my head. I leaned forward and said to the taxi driver, in the friendliest voice I could make, "Apek*, can change the station or not? Change song please?" I did this because I knew that Maria had worn her tudung for her interview.

Paya Lebar, 8 PM

His favourite spot again: right at the top of the stairs, a blind ending where there is a metal ladder leading up to a trapdoor to the roof. The trapdoor is padlocked, but his mischief on Thursday nights does not involve trespass, but truancy. He has smuggled comic books in the satchel along with his Quran and its support, the rehal (the Quran should always be elevated, and if one were to drop it, one should bring it to touch the chin, then nose, and then forehead, a ritual action performed three times).

When he returns home an hour later, he will tell his parents that Pak Haji has allowed him to advance by a few more pages, and will show the new position of the satay-stick pointer as evidence. He will not know that they have already received a phone call regarding his absenteeism. They will extract the tearful truth from him by making him swear with his hand on the Quran, a book he has hardly read but whose mysterious holiness, to an 11-year-old, was incontestable.

Gravity

Every Sunday Badron would arrive at his ex-wife's place in Yishun to pick up his daughter. It was actually his in-laws' place—he had sold their house after the divorce, and the ex-wife had decided to move into her parents' flat.

At 9.05 AM, he received an SMS telling him that he could collect Atiqah. He took the lift up and walked down two flights of stairs. When he reached the door, the gate was already open. Atiqah was wearing a white dress, printed with pictures of pairs of cherries.

"That's a pretty dress," he said to her. Atiqah's face beamed with pride. "Did you choose it all by yourself?" he asked.

"I wanted the one with strawberries," she replied.

His ex-wife interjected, "They didn't have her size. The ones they had were all too small."

Badron detected a note of defensiveness in her voice. "But this one is very pretty also," he said, stroking Atiqah's hair.

"Where are you taking her today?" the ex-wife asked.

"There's a toy fair at the Expo."

"Toys again? She's five already. Why don't you buy her storybooks?"

"Good idea," he said, smiling at his ex-wife. She looked away. Badron looked down at Atiqah and said, 'We'll buy toys and storybooks OK?"

It was going to be a long train ride to the Expo. Badron had wanted to take the taxi, but decided that he should save the money instead and spend it on a toy that Atiqah really liked. As someone who only saw Atiqah once a week, he felt that he did not have his ex-wife's right to subject the girl to hard-headed compromises.

On the train, Atiqah would repeat the names of the stations, which were recited with clockwork cheer by a female voiceover. When the train slipped underground from Bishan to Braddell, Badron could sense her excitement, as she knelt on the seats and cupped the sides of her face with her hands. The train entering the tunnel was an event as momentous as an eclipse, the fluorescent lamps streaking past in the whooshing darkness a parade of comets. At the City Hall interchange, Atiqah asked him whether he knew how to tell when the train was arriving.

"You can find out from the screen up there," he said.

"No," Atiqah replied, stretching the 'o', giving the word the patronisingly patient inflection of a kindergarten teacher. She leaned close to the platform doors. "If you put your ears here, you can hear the wind. Then you'll know it's coming."

At the Expo, they were greeted by a man who was passing out helium balloons. Atiqah picked out a pink one, printed with the words 'Toy Expo 2011'. She grinned widely as Badron wound the string around her hand.

"Hold it properly, OK?" he told her. Then he flicked the balloon with his finger, such that it bobbed to the side. The balloon quickly righted itself, like a stick-figure sentry offended at having to deviate from its dignified station.

They wove their way around the various display booths, and once in a while Badron would try to get Atiqah interested in a doll, a miniature plastic tea-set, or a bucket of building blocks (priced under his limit of twenty dollars). But she seemed to be very distracted, as if she had decided that the target of their excursion was not the purchase of a toy but the visiting of every single booth in the hall. Upon reaching a booth, Atiqah's eyes would glaze over, and she would immediately point to their next pit-stop.

After half an hour of entertaining Atiqah's erratic spurts of attention, Badron started to get restless. She dismissed all his suggestions, often without properly inspecting the box or plastic casing that he knelt down to present to her. Badron wondered if Atiqah behaved this way with his wife on their shopping trips. But had she not told him how she had picked out a dress for herself? Why then was she so indifferent to all these toys?

Badron was struck by a tender delusion: maybe Atiqah assumed that once they had bought the toy, then their trip would be over. Perhaps this was her way of prolonging the time spent in her father's company. He found himself momentarily paralysed in reverie: how did he manage to bring a life into this world, only to split that life later on into half? Were his visits a welcome break in Atiqah's routines, or were they actually inconvenient interruptions?

"Ayah!" cried Atiqah suddenly, and Badron swivelled round to see her looking upwards, distraught. The balloon had escaped. Without thinking, Badron jumped up and stretched out his hand, but to no avail. The balloon kept on ascending, aloof, insensate to the loss that was swelling in its wake. A slight breeze made its trajectory slightly diagonal, and the high ceiling prevented it from travelling any further.

It was as if the balloon had finally found a place of rest, a place to fall asleep.

"Ayah, I want my balloon back," Atiqah pleaded.

"We'll go and get another one for you," Badron replied. "The same colour, OK?"

"But who's going to bring it down? Is it stuck there? It's so high up, Ayah. Can anyone climb that high?"

"It'll come down, Atiqah. You don't have to worry."

"How?"

Badron felt too tired to explain. The balloon will shrink over time. It will one day end up on the floor, and a sweeper will whisk it into a dustpan. There was something in that image which made Badron suddenly indulge in self-pity. Why did he think he had divided Atiqah's life into half? He did not even have half to claim. He was a weekend father. All he had was one seventh of her entire week. Less, actually: six hours with her each time. Who knew if he would take up even less space in her life as the years wore on? He looked at his watch. It was already past eleven.

Atiqah was still looking at the ceiling. "Atiqah, look here," Badron said. "Look at Ayah. I'll get you another balloon. Let's go, sayang. Or we'll be late."

Singapore By Night

He didn't know when exactly the name 'Bob' started to stick to him. It could have been when he first started helping out as a sound crew member at gigs. 'Bob' was actually more of a designation than a nickname. It was used to describe any Malay guy who was a little on the plump side, dark-skinned, and who was involved in audio engineering. Interestingly, if a 'Bob' was more plump than usual, he would be called 'Bobo'.

Bob first met Suzanna during a concert for local acts at the Outdoor Theatre at the Esplanade. She was the frontwoman for an all-girl band called Fairydustball, which performed songs that were mainly ambient music, punctuated by minimal lyrics, recited over and over again. Suzanna had a breathy, little-girl voice, and when she stood on stage, assumed the vulnerable, knock-kneed posture of the ingénue.

It was a particular form of showmanship; refusing to project one's self towards the audience but instead drawing them in towards a private, pinprick space, the space of the terse, cryptic diary entry, or a hairline crack in the heart. In fact, for most of her songs, Suzanna would avoid eye contact with the audience. Hers was a solipsistic but yet strangely magnetic performance, declaring to the audience the fact that she wanted to be understood as an enigma.

During the post-show supper, Bob spotted Suzanna sitting at a table just beside his. He leaned over and said, "I like what you guys did just now. It was refreshing." Bob knew that he was not entirely telling the truth. He had seen many acts like hers before, with that anxiety to claim indie cred cleverly disguised as nonchalance towards populist antics. And honestly, a couple of Suzanna's songs teetered dangerously between the whimsical and twee.

Suzanna smiled. She had a dimple only on her left cheek, and that kind of asymmetry (what happened to the missing dimple on the right?) gave her beauty a mysterious edge. Bob asked who her favourite singers were.

"I kind of like Cat Power," she said. "Feist is all right."

"What about closer to home?" Bob asked.

"Oh. I think Yuna's not bad. And Zee Avi. They're bringing a different sound to the scene. Because they're not belters. Not like Siti Nurhaliza. Or Ning Baizura. And that Dayang..."

"Dayang Nurfaizah? She's got that whole R&B thing going on."

"Yeah," said Suzanna. "I don't get why she's trying to sound so black. But what about your favourite singers?"

Bob thought for a moment. He had already told one white lie. He decided that he should not inaugurate an acquaintance with Suzanna with a whole series of them.

"I like Saloma," he said.

"Saloma? You mean, like P. Ramlee's wife?"

"Kartina Dahari was once asked who her favourite singer was. And she said Saloma."

"Kartina who?"

"How can you not know Kartina Dahari? She's from Singapore also."

"You mean Saloma was from Singapore too?"

"She grew up in Pasir Panjang. Actually four of my favourite singers are all from Singapore. Saloma, Kartina Dahari, Rafeah Buang and Sharifah Aini. And you know the interesting bit? Saloma's Malay, Kartina is Javanese, Rafeah is Bawean, and Sharifah is Arab. And they all produced amazing Malay music."

"Wow," Suzanna said. "You listen to all those old songs?"

"I was looking for songs about Singapore one day. And then I came across this song called 'Keroncong Singapura'. It's also known as 'Singapura Waktu Malam'. By Saloma. You want to have a listen?"

"Sure."

Bob took out an MP3 player from his bag. He was always excited to share music with others, because it allowed him to rediscover them anew, through another person's ears. And then of course there was the image of Suzanna and him, their ears linked by an earphone wire. Its dimensions would force them into a specific proximity with each other; not too close such that their shoulders would touch (no, not yet at this point), but not too far as to stretch the wire to a state of precarious tension.

The song was played. Bob wondered whether Suzanna was familiar with the keroncong, that Indonesian musical style consisting of intricate, interlocking melodies made by a flute, guitar, a pizzicato cello or string bass, and of course the keroncong itself, a ukulele-type instrument. The Portuguese were the ones who introduced that small guitar, adapted later by the Indonesians and also Hawaiians. And the sound it produced was a distinctively island sound; combined with the flute, it evoked languor and listlessness, the strumming of coconut fronds by the sea breeze.

Later on, Bob explained to Suzanna how the keroncong, for him, was the meeting point between two maritime peoples, the kinship between the Portuguese saudade and the Malay rindu, both words which express a longing inexpressible in other languages. And 'Singapura Waktu Malam', sung in 1962, was not just about a private yearning but a political one— he wish to merge with the Federation of Malaysia. There were those lyrics, for example:

Prosperous Singapore
Peaceful and harmonious
Becoming richer by the day
As part of Malaysia

"These days, the only songs with the word 'Singapore' in the lyrics are National Day songs," Bob said.

"I'd like to listen to more of these songs," Suzanna said. And so they exchanged numbers. Suzanna insisted that Bob enter her name as 'Suzy' in his phone. Over the next couple of weeks, Bob would chat with her whenever he saw that she was online, and send her his favourite songs. He sometimes wished that he was still living in the 50s', where music was not so easily digitised and transferable. He would have liked to pass her vinyl records instead, because that would have necessitated a meeting.

One night, Bob decided that he would not lie to himself anymore. He was falling for Suzanna, and so he sent her an SMS with the word 'rindu'.

"What?" came the reply.

"I miss you. I wish we could see each other again. When I first saw you on stage that night I knew you were...the one for me."

There was no reply from Suzanna's side for a full five minutes. And then his handphone beeped.

"Bob, I'm so sorry. But I don't even know your real name."

"You never asked me."

"I think that says it all, right? If I felt the same way about you, I would have asked right from the start."

Bob switched off his handphone. At some point during the past two weeks he had fantasised: Bob and Suzy. Those would be their pet names for each other. It was just like P. Ramlee and Saloma, calling each other 'Remy' and 'Sally'. He would listen to Saloma again. That voice of hers: so light and clear, but not airy, the vowels causing each word to expand like blown glass, given shape and weight. It would be the perfect lullaby. All he wanted to do now was to fall asleep.

Singapore by night
With its twinkling neon lights
Its tall glittering stores
Resplendent beyond compare

It has been written since long ago
Singapore has never been short of stories...

Visitors

Hidayah tried every means to dissuade her parents from visiting her in New York, but nothing seemed to work. Her father had recently retired from his job as a primary school teacher, and therefore could draw on his pension to afford the trip. She could not offer the alternative suggestion that they use the money to fund their pilgrimage to Mecca, since they had already performed the Haj four years ago.

"You sound like you don't want us to come and see you," her father said.

"It's very cold here, Abah°."

"I don't hear your teeth chattering over the phone."

"That's because I'm indoors."

"So we'll stay indoors too when we get there."

"What's the point of a holiday if you're just going to stay indoors?"

It was actually the summer holidays, so Hidayah was not being completely honest when she said that it was going to be very cold. The temperature would range between 25 to 30 degrees. However, Hidayah rationalised, this would still be colder than what her parents were used to in Singapore.

Hidayah wasn't so sure why she resisted so strongly the idea of her parents' visit. Her housemate, the only daughter of a property tycoon, had decided to spend her summer back in Hong Kong, but had generously offered to cover her half of the rent for a whole four months. Which meant that there was accommodation available for Hidayah's parents, and she did not have to put them up at a hotel.

Maybe it was because she had already planned her summer itinerary. She had secured a job at the campus bookstore, and was looking forward to making acquaintances with other New Yorkers and exploring the city after hours. She had only spent one semester here, and felt that she was still in a period of adjustment.

In her class for example, Hidayah often struggled to describe herself to others. Some of her classmates thought she was Filipino, while others assumed she was Latino. When she mentioned that she was from Singapore, there was a momentary look of understanding on their faces, which Hidayah knew was actually a misunderstanding. The next minute would be spent explaining that Singapore was not part of China, was nowhere near Hong Kong or Taiwan, and that she was not Chinese.

Her classmates who were a little bit more well-travelled had a conception of Southeast Asia, but even then it was limited to the holiday bacchanals of Bangkok and Bali. And then when she also revealed that she was Muslim, she realised that this also required re-orientation: steering them away from what they knew of Islam in the Middle East, or the subcontinent. Ultimately, when she told them that she was Malay, this was often accompanied by another round of clarifications—that she wasn't Malaysian and that she wasn't of immigrant stock. "Even if my ancestors came from Malaysia," she would say, "you don't call it migration when all you have to do is cross a narrow straits".

Even then, some of her classmates would mispronounce

the word later, saying 'Mah-lay' or 'May-lay'.

Hidayah decided that in New York, to introduce herself was not simply a matter of description, but also explanation. She often wondered whether she could somehow combine the two. Perhaps the secret lay in the order in which she presented herself: as Asian, Malay, Muslim, Singaporean. There were sixteen different permutations of the order in which those four categories could be announced. Surely one of them would make sense in New York.

Given this backdrop, Hidayah wondered how comfortable her parents would feel in the city. Of course New York was quite possibly the most cosmopolitan place in the world, and people in general did not display any provincial curiosity towards outsiders. And yet at the same time, she wished that there was some familiar enclave that her parents could retreat to once the city's dazzling diversity began to glare into their eyes—a place like Chinatown or the Jewish Lower East Side. The Malay diaspora, to the best of Hidayah's knowledge, was confined to the Cape Malays in South Africa, the Ja Minissu of Sri Lanka, and the Javanese descendants of contract workers in Suriname.

So much would be novel for her parents in New York. Hidayah was anxious that she herself would not be seen as part of that novelty. She knew that her wardrobe had changed in response to the city's climate, but there might be other aspects that were invisible to her, such as a new accent, or a certain posture or attitude that she adopted in public: less deferential, less of the wide-eyed newcomer sending out pheromones to potential muggers. She dreaded being quizzed on her knowledge of the best halal eating places around town (she often made do with kebabs and salads) or even where the nearest mosque was.

Weeks breezed by, and one evening Hidayah found herself at the arrival hall of the John F. Kennedy International Airport. And then she spotted them: her father was wearing a blue windbreaker, and her mother a beige cardigan. Her mother also had a pink tudung on, printed with white flowers. Hidayah had never seen her parents dress with all that outer clothing before, and she wondered if their frugality had made them borrow from friends or relatives, rather than purchase new sets.

When they saw her, Hidayah's parents smiled. Hidayah remembered how when she was younger, her father would always call her out from her room when there were visitors to their house. He would knock at her door and insist that Hidayah appear in the living room to salam the guests. Hidayah sometimes resented the ritual, because not only was she shy, but sometimes she felt like an exhibit meant to demonstrate courtesy, gleaming proof of parenting skills.

Now, however, this seemed like the most natural thing to do. A few passersby looked on curiously as Hidayah took hold of each of their right hands in turn, bent down slightly, and pressed it to her nose. It could have been something self-conscious to Hidayah—a performance of an aspect of her own culture, a culture she had been at pains to define to others.

But it was a private gesture to her, a way to reconcile the solemnity of respect with the tenderness of affection. (The bow was too formal, the hug too intimate.) She recalled sometimes wanting to salam her mother before leaving the house, only to be told that her mother's hands were smelling of fish (which she had just scaled). But Hidayah would do it anyway. This time, however, both her parents' hands smelled like moisturiser, applied to stave off dryness in the aeroplane cabin, during that 18-hour journey that they took just to see her.

Kampung Glam, 10 PM

The waiter placed another ember—a jewel clasped between tongs—on the tinfoil of the shisha pipe. Under the shadow cast by a shophouse, a group of young boys were trading stories about their respective national service camps. Not all of them had been enlisted into the army; some of them had been drafted into the Police Force, or the Civil Defence Force.

They told stories about sadistic superiors, obtuse buddies, and eccentric bunkmates. They compared the quality of the food served at their cookhouses, the strenuousness of their training, the privileges—or rather, concessions—they enjoyed, described by the term 'welfare'. Certain characters recurred: the suspected homosexual, the academic overachiever who faked depression, the gang leader chafing at authority, and the tough-as-leather non-commissioned officer who was like the foul-mouthed uncle they all wished they had.

Huddled on an Oriental carpet, they spun fabulous tales, dreading the next morning, their exit from what they now understood as civilisation. Two years, discounting weekends and the time to clear their leave—the sum of it all was still, at the very least, more than 600 barbarian nights.

The Borrowed Boy

When Junaidah entered the orphanage, she could not help but feel expectant. It was just as well that her husband and Haikel preferred to remain in the car. She would be the first point of contact into the family, and despite the fact that she was not a man, she hoped that he would somehow stick by her side for the rest of the day. A woman in a cream tudung was waiting at a counter, which was decorated with ketupat° woven from shiny light green ribbons. There were children's drawings on the noticeboard, many of them filled with the words 'Selamat Hari Raya'. Junaidah noticed how they were filled mostly with pictures of children, not families. But at least the children were smiling.

After Junaidah had introduced herself, the receptionist checked a list and said, "You're the one who wanted an eight-year-old boy, right?" Junaidah wondered if her request had been exceptional, and immediately felt apologetic. She did not want to come across as someone prone to unreasonable demands. The receptionist smiled and said, "I'll go and bring him down. They're all upstairs right now. They've just had their breakfast. We had lontong° and rendang° today. You know lah, once a year. Why don't you take a seat first?"

Junaidah sat down on a leather sofa. There was a crater in one of its armrests, exposing the beige sponge padding inside. Someone, probably a child, had been picking at it, fingernails burrowing through the sponge either out of nervousness or boredom. She did not expect the orphanage to look like a school, with two flags at a quadrangle near the façade, and three storeys of what could have been classrooms—except that they were dormitories.

It was a good idea to have them sequestered upstairs. Junaidah had feared having to pass through the faces of children, their hopefulness on her way in, their disappointment on her way out. She wondered if she might have asked for another child, and another, just enough to fit into the car.

Was it not somewhat cruel, to choose one over the rest? Except that the orphanage had chosen for her. Perhaps this was a reward for good behaviour, to be hosted by a family for a day. Junaidah felt comforted by the idea that she was merely a host, and that the child was her guest. Her role today was to be defined by hospitality, not the construction of an intricate fantasy. She was not going to pretend that the boy was her son; neither should the boy believe that this family setup was anything more than temporary.

Junaidah had to admit that she had not always been so circumspect. When she had watched that TV magazine programme during the fasting month, the one that showcased the children at the Darul-Ihsan orphanage, it had affected her so much that she could not sleep properly at night. It made her cry just to relate the story to her husband when he later got home from work: all those children without parents, whose Hari Raya would painfully remind them only of what they lacked, no jars overflowing with cookies and biscuits, no filling their pockets with crisp, folded dollar notes, a festival of absence. Her family members didn't know how fortunate they were, it was an obligation to let others partake of their privilege.

The next day, she called the orphanage, asked them about the scheme where families could volunteer to provide selected children with a 'real Hari Raya experience', and signed up. When she put down the phone she was flushed with that superior happiness that comes about from making other people happy.

The receptionist returned five minutes later with the boy. His name was Mydeen, and she spelt it out for Junaidah, a unique English spelling for a name otherwise recognized as 'Maidin' or 'Maideen'. He was dark, a Jawi Peranakan child, of Indian Muslim and Malay extraction. Junaidah did not know many Jawi Peranakans, but it sometimes amused her how the 'i's' in their names became 'ee's': Fateema, Jameelah, Lateef.

Mydeen looked at the floor shyly as the receptionist spoke. She told Junaidah that he was in Primary Two, a badminton player, and that he was quite reserved. He was wearing his pink satin baju kurung, a colour that clashed with his skin tone. Junaidah noticed his thick, well-shaped eyebrows, his high cheekbones, and a sharp, almost hooked nose. He was tall for his age, and while Junaidah believed eight-year-olds were still amorphous, she could already see how this one's features could step out of the haze of youth and solidify; he would turn out to be quite a handsome young man.

"Have you eaten?" Junaidah asked him.

"Yes."

"Was it nice?"

Mydeen nodded. And then he reached out and slipped his hand into Junaidah's. She was shocked by the intimacy of the gesture, and thought to herself: *He must be impatient to get out of here.* Junaidah signed a few forms briskly, thanked the receptionist, and walked out of the building with Mydeen.

On her way out, she considered the possibility that the act of taking her hand was something almost reflexive for him, having been fostered out to different Hari Raya families year after year.

So she had been mistaken about the automatic hand-holding, a gesture not of animal instinct or need but habit and perhaps even calculation. *I'm not the first*, Junaidah thought to herself. A moment later she found herself beaming in the direction of the family car, beaming to hide her disappointment, beaming as if amused at why she would feel any disappointment in the first place.

Playback

After the song had finished, Pak Khairi stood in a daze, his hand clasped around the karaoke microphone, as if it was his only grip on reality. He had not uttered a single word during the song, even though he knew the lyrics by heart and did not need the captions to guide him. Instead of a ball bouncing over the words to mark the tempo, a wipe of yellow had bled across the letters from left to right.

His son was in the video; his son, who had left home two years ago.

His son had graduated with a diploma from a local arts college, and had been involved in some amateur stage productions with a theatre company that was based at a community centre. Pak Khairi attended one of their productions, and was puzzled by what he watched. The stage was bare, with the exception of three white cubes. Ropes were dangling from the flybars, which made Pak Khairi anxious as to whether anyone would attempt to climb them.

The actors declaimed their lines to the audience, in a lyrical but ponderous Malay. His son was a member of the supporting ensemble, and Pak Khairi was embarrassed during scenes when the boy would writhe on the floor or freeze, his arm outstretched towards the spotlight. Pak Khairi could not conjure sufficient suspension of disbelief to follow the narrative. He was often distracted by the fact that there was too much unnatural strain in their bodies and voices, by the sweat on caked foreheads and the extravagant spray of spittle ejected during violent monologues.

After the performance, his son had asked Pak Khairi what he thought of it. And all Pak Khairi could think of saying was, "So did the main character take his own life at the end?" His son had tried to explain that it was something the audience was supposed to decide, but for Pak Khairi this only meant that the work was unfinished. It had ended with a cliffhanger, like those drama serials on television. Pak Khairi also thought that if there was indeed a sequel to the play that might resolve his question, it was unlikely that he would watch it. But he did not voice this aloud to his son.

His son was soon auditioning for roles in TV dramas, though with little success. He first attended casting calls for the Malay TV station, and then decided to try his luck with the English TV station. Pak Khairi could not hide his frustration with what he saw as his son's obstinate delusions.

"What do you think you can do on Channel 5? Act as a policeman? Even someone as handsome as Aaron Aziz ends up playing a policeman."

"They have all kinds of roles on TV, Bapa°," his son replied.

"The only way you can make it big on TV is if you join Singapore Idol. Ah, that one, you can have Malay boys winning. Because it's not them who decide. It's decided by voting. But the problem is, you cannot sing."

Their quarrels became more frequent, more lacerating. As a widower, Pak Khairi missed having a woman's touch around the house. He wanted his son to get married as soon as possible. But to settle down he had to first secure a proper job.

"Know your place," Pak Khairi told his son one day.

"What do you mean?"

"This stupid dream of yours, you can't go anywhere with it. Not in Singapore."

"Then maybe Singapore is not my place."

Within the week, his son had packed up his bags. He was leaving for Kuala Lumpur. And after an absence of two years, he had returned, back to the living room, in a karaoke video. Was this what his son had meant by there being more opportunities for him across the causeway? So as to end up moving ghost-like across the screen, as much of a backdrop as the jetty, the wooden railings, the lethargic waves lapping the shore? An empty image, to accompany other people's rendition of another artist's song?

Another insult, in fact a sad parody: the song was by Ramli Sarip, one of a handful of Singaporean singers who had actually gained fame in Malaysia. And here was his son, another Singaporean, with less talent and less luck, lip-synching to the man's song. Pak Khairi decided to start the song again. His son appeared, wearing a brown baju kurung and a songkok. He had gained a little more weight since Pak Khairi had last seen him; his shoulders were broader, and his cheeks were not sunken—a sign that he was not dabbling with drugs. He was walking along a beach, and they had used a graded vermillion filter to suggest a sunset. Or a sunrise. The intro ended and the song began:

I who am still journeying through life
So long lingering at the world's crossroads

Travelling across roads and bridges

Forests and oceans

Searching for something everlasting

Pak Khairi started to sing along to the second verse. He thought of all those old Malay movies, often punctuated with musical numbers. Momo Latiff had lent her voice to Siput Sarawak. Nona Asiah to Zaiton, Aziz Jaffar to Ahmad Mahmud, Abdullah Chik to Nordin Ahmad. This was a convention borrowed from Indian cinema, where a playback singer provided the vocals to a film star. But to the audience watching a movie, enraptured by its illusions, voice and body were one.

Two Brothers

Helmy, my older brother (by ten minutes), arrived one Saturday evening in a brand new BMW, in gleaming gunmetal blue. He was taking us—our parents and I—for dinner at a buffet restaurant near Outram. His number plate, however, was the same one he had for his previous car, beginning with the letters 'WMD'. It was a joke he never tired of telling: that the Americans were looking in the wrong place for weapons of mass destruction in Iraq. They should have tried the suburbs of Taman Tun Dr Ismail instead.

At the restaurant, which served Indonesian cuisine, Helmy mentioned how difficult it was to get good Malay food in Singapore. He told us of spreads where they served twenty varieties of ulam, or Malay raw salad. He spoke about nasi kerabu, that Malaysian East Coast delicacy consisting of rice that was tinted blue from butterfly pea flowers.

"The next time we go to KL," he said, "remind me to take you to eat at Kampung Baru."

Helmy has been trying to persuade us to relocate to Kuala Lumpur ever since he received his Malaysian PR° three years ago. He had been working as an account manager for a private television station for ten years prior to that, and was now making his exponential ascent up the corporate ranks. I, on the other hand, was working as a documentary cameraman in Singapore.

While sipping from a glass of avocado juice, Helmy said, "I thought you were going to send me your résumé."

"I haven't had the time yet," I replied.

"The last time I asked was three months ago," he said.

"I've been busy. We just shot a documentary in Medan last month."

"I've already prepared the letter of recommendation."

I could see that our parents were shifting uncomfortably in their seats. They knew how much I resented Helmy trying to dispense favours, which was his way of asserting his big brother superiority (and trying to exaggerate what was a negligible headstart in life). I knew better than to start picking a fight with him over dinner. At the same time, I could not resist correcting his perception that our well-being was dependent on his patronage.

"I've told you before," I said. "I don't need you pulling strings for me."

"Someone at your age would be a producer already by now," he said.

"But I don't like producing. I like being on the ground. I like working with equipment."

"Can we just have a quiet dinner, for once?" my father interrupted. "You shouldn't be quarrelling in front of food."

Later that night, after our parents went to sleep, Helmy approached me in the living room while I was watching a DVD. I muted the sound and watched him as he sat in an armchair beside me, holding a cup of coffee in his hand.

"Mak told me about what happened on the bus," he said.

"It's an isolated incident," I said.

"It's going to become more common."

"How do you know?"

"Hazry, listen to me. This place is changing. It's not the same place we grew up in. Did you ever think they'd hire bus drivers from China one day? Who can't even speak a word of English? How is someone like Mak supposed to ask for directions? Do they expect us to pick up Mandarin?"

"There's nothing wrong with learning a new language."

"You know when Mak and Ayah lived in the kampung, they spoke to their Chinese neighbours in Malay. And for our generation, we used English. What do you think the next generation will use? They're creating this environment where you'll lose out if you don't speak it. And they're using market forces to do this. They're importing monolingual speakers to put pressure on us."

"They're cheap labour, Helmy. That's all. You're reading too much into it."

"Then what about that whole policy to keep the Chinese in Singapore at 75 percent? Because they have the lowest replacement rate, then their numbers need to be topped up by the Chinese from overseas. So what does that say to you? Which comes first then? Being Singaporean or being Chinese?"

"I heard that in Malaysia, it's easier to become a resident if you're Indonesian."

Helmy stirred his coffee and sipped from his cup. I wondered whether he had trouble sleeping at night, like me. Sometimes, after tossing and turning, I would make myself a cup of coffee and cross the threshold to definite wakefulness. It was better to be awake and get some work done (for me, mostly reading or watching DVDs) than to work myself to a state of sleep. I looked at Helmy's face, trying to spot the telltale dark circles that greeted me in the mirror as dawn broke.

"We're the same, Hazry," he suddenly remarked. It was as if he had read my mind.

"What do you mean?"

"I used to think that things were different in Singapore. I thought we had different rules, different standards. But I realised we're the same. When it comes down to it, it's all about race. Sons of the soil, sons of the Yellow Emperor. They're just the same. But being the same doesn't mean being equal. Either dominate or be dominated."

"So you go to where you can dominate?"

"There's no future for us in Singapore."

"Helmy, our past is in Singapore."

"What past are you talking about? Look at what happened to the Malay Settlement in Eunos. To the Istana Kampung Glam. To Bidadari."

"So if we all leave, then who's going to stay behind?"

Helmy sighed. "You're always the sentimental one."

"And what about you?"

"I'm pragmatic, Hazry."

"That's very Singaporean of you, Helmy. Maybe you're much more Singaporean than you think," I said.

Helmy smiled, and took another sip from his cup. I knew that no more words on the matter needed to be exchanged, for now at least. A kind of silence had begun to settle between us, a silence that could either mean an impasse, or a truce.

Kallang, 12 Midnight

Three days after her mother's funeral, she discovers the exercise book on top of the refrigerator. It is filled with recipes that were copied from the radio. The penmanship is small, cursive, but neat, and it must have taken a certain degree of skill to write at the speed at which the radio announcer recited ingredients and instructions. She feels a certain grief as she leafs through the yellowing pages, mottled at the edges; this is the only evidence of her mother's writing, and even then, it's all dictation.

Had her mother ever unburdened herself in a letter? Would it be absurd to speculate if her mother had ever written a poem? Used exclamation marks? What kind of testimony is this, in ounces and teaspoons?

When her sister walks into the kitchen, she tells the latter of her dismay. Her sister shakes her head and replies, "Just because she never wrote doesn't mean she never found ways to express herself. What do you think she put into her cooking? What you're reading is only half of it. The rest was her."

A Starry Hill

During their school holidays, Shazeela and Nurdiyana always made it a point to visit Kuala Lumpur. They would save up for the coach ride and a three-night stay at a modest three-star hotel.

Kuala Lumpur was different without their parents around. They would not have to tail them on trips to handicraft markets, where their mothers would coo over gaudy batik scarves, or eat at 'Western' restaurants that were not halal in Singapore, their fathers enthusing over grilled steaks and roast chicken.

There was something provincial about their parents' conception of Kuala Lumpur, which was perceived as a place of both familiarity (everyone spoke in Malay), as well as freedom (there were few dietary barricades). But the girls knew that the place wasn't just an expanded Geylang Serai bazaar. There was a pulsing energy to the city, and a dizzying cosmopolitanism that they could not find in Singapore. Once, after jaywalking in front of the Pavilion Shopping Mall, they found themselves assailed by a sight they could not make sense of: Iranian women in chadors, Burmese men in cleaning services polo tees, towering Scandinavian backpackers.

The girls also felt that the nightlife in Kuala Lumpur held more promises of nocturnal adventures (cars audaciously parked on pavements, faces of indeterminate ethnicities). One of their favourite spots was the Bukit Bintang stretch. Since they were not locals, the name still retained its etymological innocence, and its very mention enchanted them, conjuring up a hill which people climbed to gaze at stars.

One night, the girls decided to check out a bar at Changkat Bukit Bintang, which a website guide described as having a 'mixed expat and local crowd'. The girls had spent close to an hour ironing their hair, matching their clothes, ensuring that their eyeliners ended in perfect calligraphic upstrokes. After all that, they would spray perfume on themselves, to create the impression that their appearance was not deliberate and laboured; they were effortless clouds of colour and scent.

The girls always felt confident walking around Kuala Lumpur. They knew that they were attractive, but part of that confidence—or superiority—also came from a certain self-image as Singaporeans. They were certain that they had an advantage over other girls in Kuala Lumpur, like the ones who came from smallholder farms (whom they called Minah Felda*), or the 'skanky ones' who wore low-riding jeans which exposed spotty posteriors (whom they called Minah Bohsia*).

In the bar, the girls bought some soft drinks and parked themselves in a corner. The crowd was thickening, and the girls tried to be nonchalant to the glances that were darting in their direction. A group of boys appeared, and occupied the seats beside them. They were Malay youths, but well-dressed, in crisp ironed shirts (though something in their manner suggested that they did not do their own ironing). A couple of them had mixed features, with eyes and hair that would probably reveal their fiery brown hues under the sun.

After a few minutes, one of the boys turned to the girls and asked, "Can I top up your drinks? What would you like?" He was not one of the mestizos, but he was fair-skinned, with thick, inky eyebrows.

"We're fine for now," Nurdiyana replied.

"Where are you girls from?" the boy asked.

"Singapore," Nurdiyana replied, flattered that he had asked. "This is my best friend Zeela. And I'm Diyana. Are you from KL?"

One of the other boys, who was listening in, said, "He's from the Royal House of Kedah!"

The boy who spoke first frowned at this interruption. "Are you on holiday?" he asked the girls.

Nurdiyana replied that they were, and in the next few hours found out that the boy was studying at the London School of Economics, and was back for summer vacation. He bought jugs of drinks for his friends, who would wander off and come back, but who never attempted to join in the conversation with the girls. Shazeela could see that Nurdiyana was quite smitten: she recognised the forced laughter, the anecdotes she had heard before, but now polished for another airing. Shazeela assigned to herself the role of a watchful but somewhat indulgent chaperone.

When the girls left the bar, Nurdiyana showed Shazeela the name card the boy had passed her.

"Tengku Azlan," Nurdiyana said. "He said he's going to call me tomorrow."

"But we're going back tomorrow," Shazeela said.

"Maybe we can extend?" Nurdiyana asked. Shazeela did

not like the scratch of hope she detected in her voice.

But the boy did not call. Nurdiyana waited until it was time to check out, and then rang him up herself. Three times. Nobody answered her call. On the bus, she was silent, leaning back in her seat with her sunglasses on.

"You know why we keep going up?" As her eyes were shielded, it seemed as if Nurdiyana was not addressing anyone in particular. "We do it just like our parents. We go up to discover who we really are."

Shazeela wanted to feel some sympathy for her friend, but it was annoyance that she felt instead. Nurdiyana was too old to be nursing some fantasy of becoming a princess, or a member of some royal entourage. She should know better, coming from Singapore, where there were no palaces or farms, no peasants or kings. How silly these notions were!

"No," Shazeela thought, "We go up so as to discover who we are not. And we'll keep going up to discover it again and again." But she did not voice her thoughts aloud. She turned to the window, watching curtains of trees whisk by. She wondered what it would feel like to reach her hand out, through the glass, to brush her fingers against the sun-shimmering leaves.

The Boy at the Back of the Bus

When you're used to winding your way through traffic, it's natural that you tend to get quite impatient on a bus. But my car was at the workshop, and I had to find a way to get to work.

It's been a long time since I last took a bus. I found myself observing people just to pass the time. Naturally, most of them were women. The nice thing about sitting at the back of the bus is that, provided the bus isn't too full, you've actually got a catwalk right in front of you. So you console yourself like this: the bus is moving in fits and starts, but you hope that it's going to pick up some journey-sustaining beauty at one of its stops.

I usually manage to get a seat on my way to work. It's the opposite when I take the bus home. Today I was not very lucky. The bus was crammed, and the sole person who could lift my spirits was blocked by this big-sized, middle-aged man.

I didn't get a proper look at her, but the glimpses I got told me she had long, wavy hair. I also sensed that she had the kind of mysterious smile that went along with that kind of hair. Don't ask me how I knew, but I was confident that even the greatest romances began with nothing more than a hunch.

After taking the bus for a week, I've arrived at this theory. Why does everyone on public transport look so depressed? The reason is simple. Everyone's afraid of forming relationships with one another. The only person who's actively doing that is the bus driver, and that's because he's communicating with the other drivers on the road.

So when you're afraid, what you do is try to hide deep inside yourself. But when you do that, something departs from your face, a kind of layer just underneath the skin that gives it life. Maybe it's not correct to say that people look depressed. They just look depressingly blank.

And that was when I saw the kid. He was seated at the back, and he had a fishing rod resting against the window. He was a young Malay boy, wearing a singlet and slippers. He was eating keropok from one of those plastic packages that has no 'tear-here' slit so you'd have to attack it open with your own teeth.

So he was munching away, and I saw that he hadn't caught any fish (or maybe he had but let them go?). And then slowly, in the surreal fluorescent-lit interior of the slow-crawling bus, he fell asleep.

He must have been exhausted. His keropok packet was in his hands, and I was so afraid he'd drop it. His mouth was open. It was a deep sleep, and his face looked slightly pained.

I suddenly felt this terrible tenderness towards him, a kind of pity that made me forget about the girl and her never-to-be-revealed smile. I wanted to carefully extract the keropok packet from his hands, fold up the opened top and place it by his side, to wake him once he's reached his stop (somehow I would know), guarding his side and watching out at the parts of the tinted windows not plastered by ads.

I wanted, if I could, to hook a fish at the end of his line, with rainbow-coloured scales, so he would wake up from one dream and stumble in astonishment into another.

Child

i

He would insist that they sit on the upper deck. Up the spiral steps he would lead his mother, a hand on the railing, an eye on the front seats at the left side. His legs are not long enough to reach the floor, so they swing freely as the bus breaks a path through the languid afternoon. Images ripple across the windows, and he would read off street names audibly to himself and once in a while his mother would correct him. Tree branches would sweep across the roof like hairy wands. Sometimes he would thrill to the anticipation of nearing a low-hanging clump of leaflets and twigs, the sweet, triumphant crackle that would follow, and the bus, if it had a voice, exclaiming, 'I am a giant'. On the roofs of bus-stops: bottles, broken umbrellas, crushed drink cans; they are wandering souls without proper graveyards. Squinting against the sun makes him sleepy, and the shoulder next to him is a good pillow. It is a pillow that smells more of his mother than of himself though, but it is a comfort during the vertigo of sudden swervings and the drunken ambles of passengers.

When his mother tells him it is time to alight, he rushes up to the bell button and looks at her face for the signal. Any time now the bus would stop at his bidding, it is as good as a king genuflecting before him. But sometimes someone else beats him to it, and the contact between his finger and the bell withers, his arm sinks towards his side, and he scans woundedly at the faces in the bus for the adult passenger who has snatched his moment from him. All he sees is nonchalance, a bored smugness; it seems nobody succumbs to or even notices his vengeful stare. He is most angry at his mother, for not giving him the go-ahead earlier. As the bus folds its accordion doors with a hiss, she squeezes his hand and smiles sadly at him and tries to empathise with the gravity of his little mishap. But he is inconsolable. He sulks, pulls his hand away from her, folds his arms: there will be no next bus ride, there will not be another chance, he doesn't care if people are looking at him, he wants to carry a silence in him until it turns into stone. But when it is time to cross the road, his hand inches up towards hers, and he waits for another signal. "After the white van," she says. He looks up at her and is suddenly filled with love, for the sureness of her grip and for her eyes, fixed at where the horizon should be, so steely and vigilant they are almost tearful.

ii

It happens when someone steps on his Bata shoes. He would rub at the vulgar streak of dirt across the white canvas, he would steal a piece of chalk to camouflage it, before realising there are two possible shades of white. It happens also when he brings home a test paper two marks short of a perfect score; he has not yet known what it is to bear the weight of decisions, but he knows the full burden of bearing the weight of carelessness. All he wants to do is linger, take half-steps, extend time...he does this by walking tightrope along a kerb, or counting the number of steps to his second-storey flat, which to his dismay, has not changed (there are eleven, then nine). It happens also when a moment of exorbitant joy allows his arms to go unchecked, and his watch is scratched against a wall. An initial wipe erases the paint, but there is a deeper scar in the glass. Another wipe, and a trick of light, or the grease of his fingertips, almost convinces him it has disappeared. He closes his eyes, and then looks at his watch again. The scratch is still there, flashing at him, stubborn, stubborn as a heartbreak.

iii

He spends half of his weekdays in school, and this somehow splits his allegiances in half. He realises it is easier to compete with his peers than with his younger sister for attention. All it takes in the classroom is a raised arm, a correct answer, and he simultaneously becomes both the envy and the salvation of his classmates—or so he would like to think. It warms him too that the Malay teacher—herself childless, bespectacled and selendang*-wearing, with a distinguished mole on her chin, would sometimes address him as 'sayang'. In his exercise books, with ruler-guided margins and one-finger spacing between the words, this same teacher has written the word, 'baik', or 'good', over and over, and this somehow remedies each time his own mother has called him 'jahat', or 'bad', even once disowning him by relating the terrible tale of having picked him up from a garbage bin (the debt we all owe our parents is doubled when we find out that they are not our real parents).

The day arrives when his loyalties between these two women will be stretched. It is simple enough for him to take sides between groups of friends: the general hierarchy states that academic rivals are one's worst enemies, followed by girls, and then those afflicted by the sin of pride—whose new branded bag or nine-compartment pencil case are symptoms of 'showing off'. But to choose between two mothers—one stingy with her presence, the other with her praise—is much harder.

On that day, his teacher will ask the class whether anyone has a pointer to spare, and in this case she is referring specifically to one of those pointers that can be extended telescopically from what initially looks like a pen. He has seen one at the school bookshop, and his hand shoots up, almost by instinct. He cannot let anyone else usurp his position as the favoured one, and later at home, he will argue with his mother, insisting that everyone in the class is required to buy one. His mother will not be fooled; she has emptied newly-opened tissue boxes and agonised over legitimate paintbrushes (she fears some of the bristles are made of pig hair) for his Art and Craft exigencies, but this is certainly going too far. At night, he will fret over what to tell his teacher the next day. He will toss and turn on his bed, and his dream will take the shape of a train, with its wagonloads of lies (I have the pointer, the teacher says everyone must bring one to school, my mother says we've lost the pointer), an orphan train that no station will receive.

iv

He brings the consent form home from school, tucked carefully into the front pocket of his schoolbag. The phrase 'consent form' itself has always triggered off pleasant associations in him. It is not the destination that excites him—whether the Van Kleef Aquarium, the Zoo, or the Singapore Science Centre—but the thought of actually smuggling various items along for the excursion. The night before, his mother will pack for him soft drinks, a jumbo packet of Cheezels, a few Kit Kat bars and a visor (which he will not put on, since it bears the words 'PSA° Family Day'). To this list of already-contraband items (none of them are sold at his own school canteen) he will add the following: a Game-and-Watch toy called 'Hungry Giraffe' and the 'Beano' comics which were lavished upon him during his hospital stay. He knows, though, that his things might not be able to match up to the Walkmans and Transformers the others will bring; once someone had brought a hand-held basketball game which required the manoeuvring of a basketball in (real) water through the squishing of plastic buttons. Time slowed down within the aqueous court, as the mini-basketball drifted like a thistle or a feather, but it stopped for those who were gazing awestruck, crowded behind the princely game-player.

When he returns from his excursion, his mother will ask him to describe the day. He will tell her: they were given worksheets (his was only half-completed), they expected someone to fall into the eco-pond but nobody did, it threatened to rain but didn't. And what he won't: that his greatest triumph of the day was beating someone's score for a Donkey Kong hand-held game, a game that didn't even belong to him but was loaned out for a few auspicious minutes on the bus ride back to school.

Kaki Bukit, 3 AM

The rice fields were dazzling, like smooth mirrors pierced through by green stubble. He saw an egret so white it looked as if it had emerged from a sack of flour. His guardians, however, were nowhere to be seen. He thought that he should wait for them, here, on the veranda of the kampung house, whose floor was made of wooden slats. He was five years old, and he could still fit his little finger into the spaces between the slats.

Clouds had assembled, as if the sun was a bright magnet that had summoned them towards itself. It was getting dark. He climbed down the wooden stepladder and decided to look for his guardians. At the back of the kampung house, he stumbled upon a miraculous sight: a buffalo was lying on its side, ejecting from its body something which was jerking spasmodically, webbed in pink, steaming slime.

It was at this moment when he woke up from his dream. He went to his mother's bedroom and peeked in; she was sleeping peacefully. The day before, his mother had told him the story of how she was abducted by her own grandparents. Their longing for a grandchild was so great that they had brought her, without her parents' knowledge, to live with them for a week at their kampung in Rembau, Negeri Sembilan. That was where she had witnessed the birth of a buffalo calf.

Sitting in the dark of the living room, he realised how his existence did not begin only when he was born. He had always existed, in some form, before his time, in his mother's childhood. As she, in turn, would also exist, after her own time, her memories indistinguishable from his dreams.

Acknowledgements

Special thanks to Zedeck Siew for his editorial advice, Isrizal Mohamed Isa for the foreword and Ivan Heng and W!LD RICE for always giving me the space to write. Also to Khir Johari, Jamal Mohamad, Noora Zul, Alin Mosbit, Zizi Azah, Noor Effendy Ibrahim, Irfan Kasban, Amir Muhammad and Yasmin Ahmad for the inspiring conversations.

'A Hantu Tetek Story' was first published in *Silverfish New Writing 2: An Anthology Of Stories From Malaysia, Singapore And Beyond* (Silverfish Books, 2002), ed. Satendra Nandan.

'Sacrifice', 'His Birthday Present' (as 'The Birthday Party'), 'The Drawer' and 'The Convert' were first published as 'Four Women' in *QLRS* Vol. 9 No. 2, 2010.

'A Starry Hill' was first published in *Selangor Times*, 27 May, 2011.

'Overnight' was first published as 'Coast' in *Coast—A Mono-titular Anthology of Singapore Writing* (Math Paper Press, 2011), eds. Daren Shiau & Lee Wei Fen.

'The Borrowed Boy' has been expanded to a full short story and will be published in *One—The Anthology* (Marshall Cavendish International Asia Pte Ltd, 2012), ed. Robert Yeo.

About the author

Alfian Sa'at is the Resident Playwright of W!LD RICE. His plays have been translated into German, Swedish and Danish, and they have been read and performed in Singapore, Kuala Lumpur, London, Berlin, Hamburg, Zurich, Munich, Copenhagen and Stockholm. He has been nominated for the Life! Theatre Awards for Best Original Script seven times, and has received the award twice.

Alfian was the winner of the SPH-NAC Golden Point Award for Poetry and the Singapore Young Artist Award for Literature in 2001. His other publications include *Collected Plays One*, *Collected Plays Two*, *Cooling-Off Day*, the poetry collections *One Fierce Hour* and *A History of Amnesia*, and the short story collection *Corridor*.

Abbreviations and Glossary Terms

The Convert

Pg 1	baju kurung [*b.m.*]	Traditional Malay attire for women consisting of a knee-length blouse worn over a long skirt
Pg 1	songket [*b.m.*]	A hand-woven fabric in silk or cotton, and intricately patterned with gold or silver threads
Pg 1	keris [*b.m.*]	A traditional Malay/Indonesian dagger with a wavy blade, sometimes used along with ceremonial dress
Pg 1	akad nikah [*b.m.*]	Marriage solemnisation
Pg 2	kadi [*b.m.*]	An official appointed to solemnise Muslim marriages

Losing Touch

Pg 5	tudung [*b.m.*]	A headscarf worn by Muslim women
Pg 6	nak [*b.m.*]	From the Malay word 'hendak', which means 'to want'

Three Sisters

Pg 9	Mak [*b.m.*]	Mother, also used as a term of address for senior Malay women
Pg 9	jemput-jemput[*b.m.*]	Banana fritters
Pg 10	sarong [*b.m.*]	A loose-fitting skirt-like garment formed by wrapping a strip of cloth around the lower part of the body, worn by both men and women in the Malay Archipelago

Paya Lebar, 5 AM

Pg 13	Subuh [*b.m.*]	The Fajr prayers, the first of the five daily prayers offered by practising Muslims

Village Radio

Pg 15	Pok [*b.m.*]	Terengganu dialect for Pak

After The Dusk Prayers

Pg 18	Nenek [*b.m.*]	Grandmother
Pg 18	kampung [*b.m.*]	Village

Overnight

Pg 21	nasi lemak [*b.m.*]	A fragrant rice dish cooked in coconut milk
Pg 23	HDB [*l.abbr.*]	Housing and Development Board

Tampines, 7 AM

Pg 41	MRT [*l.abbr.*]	Mass Rapid Transit—a railway-based public transport system

The Morning Ride

Pg 48   Ayah [*b.m.*]   Father

Telok Blangah, 8 AM

Pg 55   Cikgu [*b.m.*]   Teacher

Litter Girl

Pg 59   I/C [*l.abbr.*]   Identity Card

A Hantu Kumkum Story

Pg 65   bomoh [*b.m.*]   A spiritual healer who practices black
                                                magic

Proof

Pg 67   Assalaamu'alaikum [*arb.*]   Greeting used among
                                                                Muslims which means
                                                                'peace be upon you'

Pg 67   ustazah   A female Islamic religious
                 [*b.m.*]   teacher

A Pontianak Story

Pg 96	Mi'raj [b.m.]	The second part of the Night Journey of the Prophet Muhammad, known as Isra and Mi'raj. During the Mi'raj (or 'ladder' in Arabic), the Prophet ascends to heaven and speaks to God, who gives him instructions on how many times Muslims must offer prayers each day

The Barbershop

Pg 99	dangdut [b.m.]	A genre of Indonesian popular music that is partly derived from Malay, Arabic, and Hindustani music
Pg 101	songkok Haji [b.m.]	A white skullcap often worn by those who have performed the Haj, or pilgrimage to Mecca
Pg 101	Mat Motors [sl./b.m]	Slang for Malay males who ride motorcycles

His Birthday Present

Pg 107	sayang [b.m.]	Love or 'my dear'

Reunion

Pg 116	keropok [b.m.]	Deep fried crackers
Pg 147	pantun [b.m.]	A traditional Malay poem, in the form of a quatrain of rhyme scheme ABAB
Pg 118	Tengku [b.m.]	A title or honorific used to denote a person of royal lineage

The Drawer

Pg 132	Mendaki [*l.abbr.*]	Yayasan Mendaki is a self-help group set up by the Malay/Muslim Community leaders in partnership with the Singapore government.
Pg 132	mee soto [*b.m.*]	Noodle soup, where the soup is made from chicken stock and spices.
Pg 133	Apek [*d.hokk.*]	A middle-aged or elderly man

Visitors

Pg 147	Abah [*b.m.*]	Father

The Borrowed Boy

Pg 155	ketupat [*b.m.*]	A traditional Malay rice cake made up of compressed rice boiled and wrapped in woven strips of palm leaf
Pg 155	lontong [*b.m.*]	A traditional Malay rice cake made up of compressed rice boiled and wrapped in banana leaf
Pg 155	rendang [*b.m.*]	A spicy meat dish

Playback

Pg 160	Bapa[*b.m.*]	Father

Two Brothers

Pg 163	PR [*l.abbr.*]	Permanent Residency

A Starry Hill

Pg 170	Felda [*l.abbr./sl.*]	Literally an acronym for the Federal Land Development Authority in Malaysia; slang to describe someone as rural and uneducated
Pg 170	Bohsia [*sl.*]	Slang for sexually promiscuous girls

Child

Pg 179	selendang [*b.m.*]	Shawl
Pg 181	PSA [*l.abbr.*]	Port of Singapore Authority, now known as Maritime and Port Authority of Singapore

Appreciation

We are very grateful to the following friends for their generous donation to Singapore Unbound's 2017 fundraising campaign.

Benefactor
Traslin Ong and Kelvin Neu

Fan
Benety Goh, Boon Hui Tan, Geoffrey Yu, Guy Humphrey, Hui Wen Lim, Karen Lim, Tim Tompkins

Supporter
Frank Pomilla, Kai Chai Yeow, Lyn Chio, Patsey Yeo-Ramaker, Paul Rozario-Falcone, Tai Ann Koh

Support Singapore Unbound.
Fractured Atlas, our fiscal sponsor, is a 501(c)(3) public charity. Contributions for the purposes of Singapore Unbound are tax-deductible to the extent permitted by law.
https://singaporeunbound.org/join-us/

About Gaudy Boy

From Latin "gaudium," meaning joy, Gaudy Boy publishes books and media that delight readers and viewers with the various powers of art.

The name is taken from the poem "Gaudy Turnout" by Singaporean poet Arthur Yap about his time abroad in 1970s Leeds, UK. Similarly inspired, Gaudy Boy seeks to bring literary works by authors of Asian heritage to the attention of an American audience.

We publish poetry, fiction, and creative non-fiction. To submit a manuscript, please query Jee Leong Koh at jkoh@ singaporeunbound.org with a book proposal.

Established in 2017, Gaudy Boy is an imprint of the literary nonprofit Singapore Unbound.

Visit our website at
singaporeunbound.org/gaudyboy